MARISSA FARRAR

TWISTED DREAMS

The Dhampyre Chronicles: Book One

Copyright © 2014 Marissa Farrar

Paperback ISBN: 978-0-9928504-7-0
Kindle ISBN: 978-0-9928504-6-3

Warwick House Press

Edited by Lori Whitwam
Cover art by Art by Karri

License Notes

This eBook is licensed for your personal enjoyment only. This eBook may not be re-sold or given away to other people. If you would like to share this book with another person, please purchase an additional copy for each recipient. If you're reading this book and did not purchase it, or it was not purchased for your use only, then please purchase your own copy. Thank you for respecting the hard work of these authors.

Publisher's Note

This is a work of fiction. Names, characters, places, and incidents are either the products of the author's imagination or are used fictitiously, and any resemblance to actual persons, living or dead, business establishments, events, or locales is entirely coincidental.

CHAPTER 1

THE POWER LINE fell from the sky in a shower of sparks, hitting the road in front of my car to lash on the asphalt like an angry snake.

My head snapped around from where I'd been gaping out of the driver's window at the scene beyond. With a gasp, I slammed on the brakes of my Audi A6, the sudden change in momentum throwing me forward. My seatbelt locked across my chest, punching the air from my lungs.

I almost hadn't noticed in time. Instead of watching the road into the small Northeastern coastal town of Sage Springs, my eyes had been drawn to the huge field to my right and the multitude of trucks and trailers parked up there. Despite the bad weather—high winds with a promise of rain—giant, brightly colored metal structures were being lifted into the air by even bigger cranes. Still lying flat on the ground were the blue, white, and red stripes of a canvas top for the carousel. Signs in garish swirls of letters, and currently unlit giant platforms of lights, also still remained on the ground, waiting their turn to be hoisted high. The field had been churned up in ruts of mud by the big, heavy wheels of the trucks. Farther in the distance, where the field turned to the asphalt of a huge parking lot which served the beach goers, some of the larger structures were already up—a huge Ferris wheel, the Waltzer, the Tilt-A-Whirl—were dotted between the smaller stands. Men in wife-beater shirts, exposed arms covered in a blur of homemade tattoos, stood shouting and gesturing instructions to the crane drivers.

I'd been watching the spectacle of the traveling carnival being raised and so hadn't noticed when something, perhaps one of the cranes or even the wind, caught the power line overhead.

On the other side of the road, dense woodland of oak and pine ran into forest, which crept inland into hilly terrain. Sage Springs was a good distance from any other town, something I'd locked into, wanting the solitude. I wasn't running, exactly. I knew I couldn't run from what I was. But I did want to leave the big city behind and start my new life at college somewhere completely different from the bright lights of Los Angeles where I'd grown up.

Far from the almost continuous sunshine of my home city, the sky was overcast here, strong gusts of wind causing the trees to bend with its force. I had been thinking that the traveling carnival shouldn't have been trying to erect such tall structures in these high winds. I guess my point had been proven.

Now my eyes were fixed on the snapped power line, still lashing around on the road. A gust of wind lifted it, causing the thrashing to grow wild. I froze inside the car, my hands locked on the steering wheel, knuckles white. The sparks died off and then spurted again like a Catherine wheel.

Was I safe inside the car? Thoughts of the rubber tires somehow grounding me went through my head, but I wondered if I might have gotten things mixed up with lightning. If the live end of the wire touched the metal shell, would it fry everything—and everyone—inside? I wanted to jump from the vehicle and make a run for it, but the high wind wasn't making things any easier. I couldn't predict which way the thrashing wire would be thrown next.

I became aware of voices, men shouting. I relaxed my grip on the steering wheel enough to turn in my seat and peer out of the rear window. Several of the men I'd been watching putting up the rides in the adjacent field had seen what had happened and come running. They gestured to each other, then to the sky where the wire had come from, and then my car.

The truth was, those men were probably in more danger than I was. I didn't know how my body would react to a severe electric shock, but I knew I'd be more resistant than they would.

Looking at the scene before me now, I worried that if this went wrong, my independent life would be over before it even got started.

The wind that had been gusting and battering the car suddenly fell still. The wire dropped to the ground, sparks still spurting, but less so now. Something drew my gaze back to the field which had first distracted my attention. In the distance stood a lone figure, a man, or boy even, dressed in black. I couldn't make out his features, but I felt certain he was watching me. I shook my head, wondering why the thought unnerved me. Of course he was. The spectacle the scene created meant everyone was watching. Yet for some reason I picked up on this person's intensity, as if his concentration on the scene was so much greater than anyone else's.

A fist thumped on my rear window, making me jump. I turned around again. The moment I did so, the wind started back up. "Hey, Miss. Get outta the car, will ya!"

Another man standing just behind him also yelled out a couple of useful comments. "What are you doing just sitting there? Back the hell up!"

I blinked, forcing myself to focus. Of course. I needed to back up to get away from the power line. I hoped no one else came along too fast behind me, or they were likely to go straight into the back of me, and force us both into the current.

As I shifted into reverse, the wire whipped in the wind, making contact with the hood. I let out a shriek, instinctively lifting my hands from the steering wheel, not wanting to touch any more of the car than necessary. Sparks exploded, the black metal of my vehicle where the exposed wire had hit turning white. Electricity danced over the shell of my car. In the engine, something popped, and instantly the car's power died, my stereo going with it. The voltage must have fried the electronics. The vehicle was a new model, so nothing worked without them.

I was stuck. My option of backing up to safety had just been taken from me.

Shit.

I forced myself to think. The electricity had traveled over the metal shell of the car, leaving me safe within. My best option would simply be sitting here and waiting for the power company to arrive and switch off the juice to this part of the grid. It might take a while and would probably make me late to register for my classes, but I figured I was better off late than dead.

The big guy who had banged on my rear window seemed to have different ideas. He strode to the car and yanked open the door. The wire lifted again in the wind.

"What the hell are you doing?" I screeched at him.

"Getting you out."

"Jesus!"

The electric cable danced. The man ducked as it flew toward him, but then another gust caught the wire, whipping it away. I knew what was about to happen. Sparks flew as the live wire spun around like a furious snake held suspended by its tail. The wire lashed directly at the guy's head. He'd been trying to save me, like I was some helpless little female, but in the end he was the one who needed saving.

Channeling all my strength, I lunged out of the open car door. My palms flattened against the man's barrel chest, and I shoved him with all my strength. He flew backward, landing on his butt before skidding and coming to a rest at the feet of his companions. At the same time, I ducked, the wire grazing the top of my head, sparks catching in my hair. I battered at my dark locks with my hands, smothering any sparks that might flare into flame. I was out now, and I saw no point in climbing back inside the relative safety of my car. Instead, I ducked low and ran toward the small crowd.

As I ran from the car, the wind gusted. Carried on the air was the scent of leather and some kind of engine oil. With it came the overwhelming feeling of being watched once again, and I didn't just mean by the men. I frowned, eyeing up the men who had supposedly come to my rescue. The scent certainly didn't appear to be anything any of them would be wearing—they appeared to be more odor de sweat and beer kind of guys. Once more, my gaze was dragged to the adjacent field, to where the boy in black remained, stock-still.

He was too far away for me to be able to meet his eyes, so then why did I feel like his were focused on me?

The boy in black wasn't the only one staring.

I could feel the group of men's eyes on me, the questions behind them. How had I managed to push my 'rescuer' like that? He was a big guy in his mid forties, with a barrel chest and a gut to match. He outweighed me three times over, but I'd sent him flying, literally lifted him off his feet, and threw him away from danger. They knew something was off, they just didn't know what.

I wasn't about to start filling them in.

The man got to his feet and rubbed the top of his head, his fat forehead pulled down in a frown of bemusement. "I must have tripped," he said, trying to explain away what had happened. "Fell over my own feet when you pushed me."

No thanks for saving your life, then?

"Sure," I said, not wanting an argument, or any further attention. "Any of you guys either handy with an engine or know of a decent garage around here?"

The carny nodded. "Micky over there can tow you. I'm pretty sure there's a chop shop a couple of miles out of town."

"Okay, great." I forced a smile. "I guess we have to wait till the electricity company shows up first."

As if they'd heard me, the wire died, the sparks fading away. We all stood, watching the end with mistrust, like a dog that might turn and bite at any moment. Several minutes passed, but nothing changed.

"We'll get you towed, Miss," the man with the barrel chest said. "Least we can do, you know, considering."

So the guy realized that had I not pushed him, he probably would have ended up hospitalized, if not dead.

"Thanks," I said. "I appreciate that."

I hoped the garage would have courtesy cars available, or I was going to be seriously late for my first day.

CHAPTER 2

I STEPPED FROM my rental vehicle, slammed the door shut behind me, and stood staring up at the red brick building that would be my home for the next four years.

The weather had brightened since I'd been towed to the garage, the sun breaking through the remaining blanket of cloud. The shop had offered me the rental until my poor, fried Audi was fixed, though they'd muttered comments about expensive cars and parts, not giving me any hope it would be returned to me soon. The replacement vehicle was a beaten old SUV, though it was probably better suited to this area than the sedan. The shiny, black chrome of the Audi would have stood out—another thing to make me feel like an outsider. While I wasn't exactly out in the sticks, people seemed to go for a more relaxed look, vehicle-wise, than the convertible and sedan-loving L.A. crowd I was used to.

At least the replacement meant I'd reached school in time

to register. I was running seriously late now, but others must have traveled as big a distance as me, if not farther, so I was sure I wouldn't be the only one to be delayed.

A big shoulder barged into mine, and I almost stumbled forward. "Wake up, dreamer!" the owner of the shoulder said as he walked by.

"Hey, watch it," I exclaimed, my forehead creasing in a frown, my body jerking away from the impact.

The person who had nudged me—a tall guy with broad shoulders and a buzzed-short blond head—threw me a grin over his shoulder as he walked away.

I scowled at his retreating back, trying not to appreciate the muscles flexing beneath his form-fitting, gray t-shirt. My first introduction to my new college and I'd already been called out on one of my flaws, daydreaming. Self-conscious, I tugged at the sleeves of my long-sleeve tee. I only hoped my other quirks weren't quite so obvious.

Most kids blame their parents for who they are. In that way, I'm no different. However, what I am is unlike any other girl starting college.

I am a dhampyre—born of a human mother to a vampire father. My parents did their best to raise me as any normal child, but hey, when your dad survives by drinking the blood of other people, something like that is always going to play on a girl's mind. Being half vampire is something I've just always known—I imagine it must be a bit like growing up always knowing you're adopted. I don't remember my parents ever sitting me down and breaking the news that I was a dhampyre to me. Boy, what a conversation *that* would have been!

I do, however, remember serious conversations about never being able to mention what my father was to anyone. I'd been warned that either he would be taken away or *I* would be taken away; neither good results in my child's mind. Oh, I'd wanted to tell people on many occasions, especially as my dad's supposed condition of extreme light sensitivity made 'vampire' the obvious taunt for kids in the schoolyard. I'd wanted them to know how close to the truth they were, for him to come and show them his speed and strength, just to shut them up, but of course that could never happen.

My existence had caused some troubles when I was younger—problems I only had a vague memory of now—and so it wasn't exactly something I wanted to broadcast. I'd even Googled 'dhampyre', hoping to get some answers, but I'd only been able to pull up fictional pages. It wasn't like a dhampyre convention occurred once a year where I could go and talk to other, like-minded, half-vampires.

In truth, the vampire side was less troublesome than whatever weird genetic screw allowed me to see things about people that hadn't happened yet. When I was younger, I struggled to tell the difference between what I actually knew about someone and what I'd picked out of mid-air. This made for some uncomfortable conversations, especially when what I'd told them came true. But lately I'd been developing an unnerving craving, one I didn't want to admit to, even to myself. If I'd admitted to either of my parents that I was craving the taste of blood whenever I became angry or upset, I was convinced they wouldn't let me move away. They'd have wanted to keep me close to keep an eye on me, and bang, there'd go my new independent life.

All around me, excited or nervous new students unloaded their belongings from their parents' cars. I could tell the parents were trying to hold it together, not wanting to cause a scene in front of their offspring's potential new friends. I recognized the tight-lipped smiles, the shiny eyes on the verge of tears, and strained expressions from the ones that had been plastered on my own parents' faces just before dawn one morning, a few days ago.

I'd made the three day drive alone. My parents had wanted to bring me, but unless we'd only traveled at night my dad couldn't come. My mom wanted to come alone, in fact, she'd begged me to let her drive up with me and fly back, but I was perfectly aware of how my mom looked. Something happened in her past which meant she regularly took drops of my dad's blood to keep her well. The result was my mother looking like a seriously hot twenty-five year old. I had no intention of watching all the guys at college noticing her before me. Beside her, I disappeared into the background.

People told me I looked like my mother, but when I stood in front of the mirror, I only saw my father staring back at me. I was blessed with my father's shock of unruly dark hair, and as for my skin, I was definitely not one to tan. Minutes in strong sunshine caused me to burn. Ironically, my dad used the excuse of xeroderma pigmentosum—a genetic disorder which made him susceptible to sunlight—to pass as a regular human. My condition wasn't so extreme, but I couldn't hang out at the beach without some serious cover-up.

People rushed past me, giving me only sideways glances as I still stood staring up at my new home. My earlier experience had left me rattled, so now nerves roiled inside my stomach, though I wasn't going to show it. The only way I dealt with being me was by toughing it out, acting as though I didn't need anyone else, as if I were fine on my own. I couldn't get too close to other people. I either saw something in their future that meant I couldn't bear to look them in the face, or I touched them and got a flash of their present. Either way, I struggled to maintain long term friendships. As for relationships with guys, well, let's just say getting physically involved with someone like me wasn't a good thing.

First thing I needed to do was register, and have my dorm and key allocated to me. Leaving my belongings in my replacement vehicle, I headed up the main path and entered the campus building. The red-brick Victorian structure managed to be both beautiful and imposing. Turrets rose from a number of points on the roof. High ceilings created a cathedral-like space. Tall, arched windows allowed the late afternoon light to filter through in beams, highlighting dust motes which spiraled lazily in the shafts.

I went to the administration office, clutching my paperwork to my chest. The door was open. A girl stood with her back to me, talking animatedly to the small woman with short gray hair who sat behind the desk, peering at the computer.

I couldn't help but eavesdrop on the conversation.

"No, Mrs. McCarthy," the girl said in curt tones. "You *do* know I am on the system because I have lived in Sage Springs my whole life, and you babysat me for half of that. You know I would not leave, which is also why you know I am on that computer somewhere!"

The poor woman behind the desk fidgeted, chewed her thumbnail, and then hit a few more keys on her computer. "I am sorry, Laurel. You're just not coming up."

The girl—Laurel—gave a sigh of exasperation, rounded the desk, and stood behind the older woman. "Up you get, Mrs. McCarthy. Time to let me have a go."

"Oh, I really don't think that's..."

"It'll be fine. No one will know."

Both their gazes settled on me loitering in the open doorway as I gawped at the gall of the new student. The girl had astonishingly blue eyes behind her glasses, her mousy blonde hair pulled up into a high ponytail. She wore an old fashioned white blouse buttoned up to the neck and teamed with jeans. Around her neck, on a chain, hung a tiny silver birdcage with a minuscule silver bird perched inside.

"She won't say anything, will you...?"

She lifted her eyebrows for me to fill in the gap.

"Elizabeth," I supplied.

"There you go," said Laurel. "Elizabeth. A nice, trustworthy name."

She gave me a wink, and I couldn't help but grin back.

"Now let me at those files." She settled in front of the computer, leaning across the administrator as she hit a number of keys, her eyes glued on the screen.

She grinned. "There you go. Told you I'd find it."

Mrs. McCarthy blinked at the screen. "But that's not the right major."

"Sure it is. I'm majoring in journalism."

"Well, no wonder I couldn't find you. I thought you were doing law to follow in your daddy's footsteps. What are your parents going to say?"

"I'm eighteen years old. They don't have to say anything."

She bristled. "I'm sure the money to pay for college has come from somewhere."

Laurel scowled. "And I'm sure that's none of your business."

Secretly, I was delighted. If this spiky girl was doing journalism, our paths would cross, either in class or on the college newspaper. I didn't know what it was, but something about her seemed different. She seemed like the type of person I could be myself around. Okay, maybe not totally myself, but the human version, at least.

The administrator printed off Laurel's schedule and handed it to her, her face taut with disapproval. I couldn't help but wonder who her parents were, if they were some kind of bigwigs in town.

Finally, Mrs. McCarthy turned her attention to me. Feeling somewhat shy about the intrusion and the tension remaining in the room, I sidled forward and pushed my own paperwork across the desk. I could only assume Laurel had arrived without any for the administrator to struggle to find her.

My details were typed in, and within a minute the printer spurted out my schedule. The older woman's warmth hadn't improved as she handed me my schedule as well, as if I'd played a part in the confrontation deliberately and hadn't simply been an accidental addition.

I smiled my thanks to her, but she'd already looked away, busying herself with something else. I mentally bookmarked her as someone I should try to avoid.

Turning from the desk, I discovered Laurel hadn't gone anywhere, but instead waited for me in the doorway.

She grinned at me and linked her arm in mine, pulling me down the corridor with her as though we'd known each other for years. I braced myself, waiting for the onslaught of images I knew would come.

Nothing happened.

"What?" she said, slowing to a halt.

I realized I was staring at her and forced my eyes away, turning my lips into a grimace of a smile. I prayed she wouldn't think I was a total weirdo. "Oh, nothing. I just thought I recognized you for a second."

She smiled. "Nope, don't think so. Not unless you've spent much time in town. I've never left."

"Perhaps it was during orientation."

She shrugged and started to walk again, though I noticed her arm slip out of mine. "Yeah, maybe. So what major did you say you were doing?"

I relaxed slightly, thankful to move onto something else. "I didn't, but it's English Lit."

"Oh, cool. We'll have some classes together then!"

"Yeah, I guess we will."

We grinned at each other, and the awkward moment melted away.

Just because I wanted to work on the newspaper didn't mean I wanted to be a journalist. I wanted to write, and I'd write anything, including factual stories. I'd already gotten in contact with the editor of the school paper, The Sage Gazette, and I reminded myself to drop in on her and introduce myself. Writing on the paper was also another way for me to fit in, to create my own niche at school. In Los Angeles, I'd always been an outsider, despite living in the city all my life. My tendency to burn instead of tan, our big, gated house in the hills, and the secretive father no one ever really saw only made me stand out as someone different. In L.A., it wasn't good to be different. This move to Sage Springs made me the outsider, but I hoped this new start would give me the opportunity to be the person I never got the chance to be back home. No one needed to know anything about my family, and the cloudier climate here meant I didn't need to slather myself in sun lotion twenty-four-seven, or make constant excuses about why I couldn't go to the beach. When I did go to the beach, I sat in a giant brimmed hat and under a couple of layers of throw overs while the other girls spread themselves out on the sand in the smallest bikinis they could find.

"You're not staying on campus then?" I asked, realizing Laurel had not been given a room key like me.

She shook her head. "No need. My folks live in town. It would be a bit weird if I decided to stay on campus when they are only around the corner. I'm hoping next year I'll be able to get an apartment with a couple of friends, but I'll have to see. I haven't mentioned my plans to my parents yet."

"How come?"

"They can be a little... overprotective."

I laughed. "Yeah, I know the feeling."

She cocked an eyebrow. "Yours too, huh?"

I nodded.

"But they let you come here by yourself?" The question was in her tone.

"I told them I'd disown them if they didn't." I could hardly tell her the truth—that my father was only capable of being protective in the night time. His attempt to be protective in the day had once almost killed him.

I was disappointed Laurel wouldn't be staying on campus, but figured we'd see each other around. I hoped my roommate, whoever that may be, was equally cool.

With my new room key clutched in my hand, I headed back out to my car to get my belongings and find my new home.

CHAPTER 3

BENDING DOWN, I heaved my huge backpack onto my back and then picked up the box containing a few of my personal items—my pillow from home, my bedside lamp, and a couple of framed photographs from my childhood. As much as I'd been desperate to get away from home, I knew I'd miss my family. But I'd spent my whole life immersed in all the fakery of the Hollywood Hills, and I'd picked this place precisely because it was so different. Sage Springs survived purely because of the college. Without the influx of students, the place would probably die away, but with the fresh injection of new blood each semester, bringing money and part time workers, the town remained vital.

I balanced the box on one arm and stooped for a third time to snatch up my laptop bag. I didn't plan on going anywhere without my baby. English Literature was my major, and my laptop was my life. If I didn't have something to write on, I'd lose my mind.

With my possessions precariously balanced, I got my feet moving and headed across campus.

My half-vampire genetics made me stronger and more agile than most five-foot-six, hundred and fifteen pound, eighteen year olds, so I strode across the lawn toward the building, not noticing the weight dragging down on my shoulders.

From the tour I'd taken earlier in the year, I knew classrooms and lecture halls filled the main building where I'd registered. The two separate buildings to the left were the boys' dorms, and the two to the right made up the girls' rooms. Each building housing the students had been named after a type of herb—I was staying in the one called Caraway. The sister building was named Loveage, while the two boys' dorms were Yarrow and Tarragon. I imagined the 'Loveage' name probably caused a few smirks and elbows jabbed in ribs for the girls who stayed there.

Of course, not everyone stayed on campus. Some lived close enough to stay home and travel in, while a few super independent types rented apartments. I wasn't anywhere close to that stage yet. Just coming here set my teeth on edge. I wanted to appear mature and brave, but my heart hammered inside my chest, and my legs felt like jelly.

Taking deep breaths, I took the path that separated a grassy knoll up to the main building and then headed right. My new building was the first. Some thoughtful person had wedged open the front doors, so I didn't need to fight with my belongings to get in. A couple of new students hung out with their parents by the elevator, and they both shot me nervous smiles. I debated waiting with them for only the briefest of seconds. I didn't want to be squished into a cramped, awkward space, and besides, I didn't tire easily, and I was only on the second floor.

Decision made, I tramped up the stairs. The door to the second floor hadn't been so conveniently propped open, so I turned around and used a combination of my elbow and back to barge through. Like a hotel, the numbers of the rooms had been engraved on a plaque on the wall. My room was number sixty-three, so I followed the brass arrows pointing me in the right direction.

I paused outside the door, which held the number correlating to the one on the key tag I now held in my hand. On instinct, I tried the handle before bothering to struggle with the key, and the door swung open.

I walked into the room to discover I wasn't alone.

"Hey!" A perfectly made-up blonde spun to meet me. A million-watt smile was plastered on her face, but I watched it falter for the briefest of seconds before she dragged herself back to little miss perfect again.

"Hey," she said again, reining in her apparent disappointment at the scruff-bag who had just imposed on her immaculate world. "I'm Brooke."

I force my own smile. "Elizabeth."

The smile remained fixed, though her eyes dropped down my body, taking in my tee and sweats. "Oh my God, that's so pretty. I just love those old-fashioned names."

Ouch, I knew it was coming. A jab in the ribs with a verbal knife.

My grin felt frozen. "Thanks." An idea suddenly occurred to me and burst from my mouth before I could stop it. "But everyone calls me Beth."

"Beth… sure," she said. "Here, let me help you with that."

"Oh, no," I shook my head. "I'm fine, really."

"Don't be silly." She reached out and grasped the sides of the box still circled in one arm. "I've got it."

Her hand brushed against mine. I got a flash of her sitting on a double bed, the coverlet beneath her covered in tiny embroidered pink roses. Her knees were pulled up to her chest as she cried into a pink stuffed rabbit—the same one, I noted, which now sat on her pillow.

I shook my head, trying to dispel the unintended invasion of her privacy. I couldn't be sure if what I'd seen came from her past or future. I wasn't sure which option I even preferred.

Unaware of my visions, Brooke took the box from me with two hands and staggered under the weight. "Jeez, what the hell have you got in here?"

Oh yeah, books. I'd forgotten about the books.

I grinned and took the box back, lifting it easily. I deposited it on the desk on the side of the room my new roommate hadn't yet occupied. Glancing over to her side, I realized she'd unpacked already. Tubes and pots of hair products, makeup and body lotions all teetered on the surface where her school work was supposed to go. A laptop with a pink cover sat unopened beside them.

"Your folks leave already?" I asked.

"Oh," she gave a shrug, her silky blonde hair sliding over her shoulders. "They didn't bother coming. They hate goodbyes and figured if I'm old enough to come to college, I'm old enough to drive myself as well."

"Yeah, me too. Welcome to our independent lives."

She offered me what I felt was her first genuine smile.

I shrugged my backpack off my shoulders and set it beside the single bed that was now mine. "So have you come far?"

"Not really. My family actually live just outside of town. They own a few thousand acres of the forests and lands west of Sage Springs."

"Oh, right," I tried to hide my surprise. She was close enough to be living at home and traveling in to school daily. "A few thousand acres? That's a lot of land."

"They own a mining company, and so they're really busy."

"Is that why you're staying on campus?"

Brooke shrugged. "I'm used to staying away. I've been at boarding school since I was eleven."

Again, I tried not to judge, but I couldn't help feeling sorry for her. As bizarre as my own family's setup was, they'd never sent me away and would have happily kept me under their roof until I turned thirty.

Not bothering to unpack, I left my stuff on my bed, made my excuses to Brooke, and headed back out.

I walked away from the dorms and went back to the central building on campus. Through the main doors, I made my way down a couple of different corridors, my shoes squeaking on the polished wood floors. I pushed open another set of heavy, arched doors and entered the place I'd been aiming for.

The accommodation for the students had been added on more recently in the history of the college, and contained none of the atmosphere of the main building. In the hushed silence of the library, I could sense the history of this place. Somewhere above my head, pipes ticked, as though the building itself had a heartbeat. This was the one part of school I'd been excited about spending time in since I'd decided which college I wanted to attend. The library not only housed my favorite things in the world—books—but was also the base for the school newspaper, The Sage Gazette. I'd applied to become a junior staff writer as soon as I'd received my acceptance letter, and I wanted to get my face in front of the Editor in Chief, Dana Trestle.

The office for the school newspaper was positioned in a far more modern room set at the back of the library. Glass walls divided it from the rest of the space, but cream blinds hung, partially open, offering the people inside a modicum of privacy. I glanced between the slats as I approached. Several desks were positioned around the periphery of the room, but only one desk had someone sitting behind it—the person, I assumed, I'd hoped to see.

Her red hair sprung in tight ringlets around her heart-shaped face. These were perfect curls, not the messy frizz I spent half my life trying to straighten out with a pair of heating irons. Her pale skin was spattered with freckles, and a pair of Ghost glasses framed her eyes. She was obviously a couple of years older than I was and seemed to be the epitome of a sophisticated woman. I suddenly became hugely conscious of the scruffy sweats I still wore and cursed myself for not changing before I came to make my introductions.

Hesitantly, my heart picking up its pace with nerves, I lifted my hand to rap on the glass door with my knuckles.

I hovered, my hand still held above the glass, as I debated going back and changing. What the hell had I been thinking anyway?

Just as I was about to step away, she lifted her head and caught sight of me.

Darn. Busted.

I continued to hesitate—did I knock now, or just go in? But she answered my question by smiling and beckoning me in with a finger.

Twisting the handle, I cracked open the door and stuck my head in. "Hi, sorry, I'm not disturbing you, am I?"

"No, not at all. I'm just catching up on some stuff. What can I do for you?"

I slunk around the door and crossed the room, my hand out. I wouldn't normally willingly make physical contact with someone new, but in this case I needed to make an impression. "Elizabeth Bandores. I'm your new staff writer."

The smile widened, revealing perfect white teeth. She slid her glasses from her nose, dropping them to her desk, and rose to meet me. I was by no means short, but she must have been close to six feet.

"Hi, Elizabeth," she said. She reached out and shook my hand. I tried to ignore the flash I got of her fighting with someone, an older man. Her father? No, he was too young. Despite the flecks of white around his temple, he didn't look anywhere near old enough to be her parent. I saw her shove him in the chest, her face streaked with tears. There was too much passion in the action for her to be related to this dark-haired man.

I dropped her hand and removed myself from her future argument—yes, future. I could see that clearly.

"Are you okay?" she asked. Clearly, I'd zoned out for a little too long. I had to watch myself.

I flashed a smile. "Yes, I'm great."

"Well, you're certainly eager."

"I am, huh? Yeah, I guess I am."

She jerked her chin toward the plastic chair set across from her, on my side of the desk. "Take a seat. You must have had a busy day."

I shrugged. "It's not been too bad. I wanted to get started."

"I'm glad you're here. I've actually got a job for you if you want to get your feet wet early. I like to get something out within the first couple of days of all you new guys starting the semester—a kind of 'welcome to Sage Springs College' edition."

I leaned forward, my elbows on my knees, my fingers laced together. "Yeah, that would be awesome."

"I need you to go and interview Flynn Matthews. Do you know who he is?" I shook my head. "He's the captain of our swim team. We're very proud of our swim team here at Sage Springs. Some of the members are potential Olympic competitors."

Inwardly, I groaned. Sports. I knew nothing about sports, especially not swimming. What the hell was I going to ask him—can you swim underwater? How long can you hold your breath? I knew I should have changed my outfit. The sweats must have made her think I'd be ideal for this assignment.

On the outside, I flashed a smile and said, "Great! I love swimming."

Where the hell had that come from?

"Cool. He'll be down at the gym. Do you know where that is?"

I nodded. I'd been shown around on the tour, though the gym certainly wasn't a place I'd ever imagined myself attending.

"You got a pen and paper handy?"

I nodded to my purse. "I always carry a notepad and pen. You never know when something inspiring might hit."

Dana grinned at me, her gray eyes lightening a shade. "You sound like my type of girl. I think we're going to get on just great, Elizabeth Bandores."

CHAPTER 4

THE SOUNDS OF the gym came muffled through the door. Feet hitting the treadmill, grunts of someone trying to lift weights, MTV on in the background. Someone brushed by me as I lurked outside. A towel was slung over the guy's shoulder as he barged through the door. The gym's noise blasted out to me before the door settled shut again.

I hopped from foot to foot, trying to build up the courage to go in.

Come on, I told myself. *This is nothing.* What if I ended up as an actual reporter and had to go to war-torn lands to get the latest story? How could I do things like that if I didn't even have the guts to walk into the college gym?

The thing was, all the people working out would be older than me—second and third years. The kids my own age were only just arriving and were far too preoccupied with settling in to bother heading for a workout.

I took a deep breath and pressed my lips together. I really needed to stop hanging around outside doors.

Letting my breath out in a whoosh, I pushed my way into the gym. Heat and the faint tang of body odor clung to the air. Everyone seemed busy with their own thing. The occupants barely glanced at me as I stood, still feeling awkward, my eyes scouring the machines. I didn't even know what the star of the swim team looked like. It wasn't as though he would be wearing a name tag.

A skinny guy in a football top about four sizes too big stopped at the water fountain to my right. He bent his head to take a drink, and the shirt ruffled up around his neck like an Elizabethan collar. He was certainly the least intimidating of the bunch.

"Excuse me?" I said. He jerked upward with a cough and a splutter. "Sorry, I didn't mean to startle you."

His eyes took me in, the briefest flick up and down my body, resting only briefly on my chest.

"That's okay," he said, his hand over his mouth to stifle another cough. "You lost?"

"No, I'm looking for Flynn Matthews. I'm a new staff writer with the Sage Gazette."

"Oh, right." His narrow shoulders dropped. "He's over here. Come with me."

My heart sank as we crossed the gym to where a guy sat on a bench, lifting weights. The moment I saw him, I recognized him from earlier in the day when he'd nudged me and asked me if I was dreaming.

"Flynn," my escort said, lifting his voice to be heard above the rest of the ruckus. "You've got a visitor."

The blond lifted his head and caught sight of me, a slow grin spreading across his face. "And there was me thinking you'd finally picked up a girl, Shawn."

A flush crept up around Shawn's throat, and I experienced a pang of sympathy for him. However uncomfortable I felt at times, it couldn't be easy being his build in a world full of jocks and gym-bunnies.

Flynn's eyes were an aqua green and incredibly sharp. I felt myself shrink under his gaze. But he kept it on my face, and I gave him credit for that. I'd been blessed with curves, and most guys checked them out before they'd even bothered looking at my face.

"You've woken up then, huh?"

I gave him a tight smile. "I was never asleep. I just like to think, that's all."

"Think or dream?"

"As long as either one uses the brain and imagination, I don't see what's the difference." I glanced down at the weights and added, "But I believe in using brain above brawn."

His eyebrows lifted at my comment. "Some people don't have a choice."

"Aren't you even going to ask me why I'm here?" I said, putting my hands on my hips.

He glanced down at the smart phone, tucked just beneath the bench, and then bent to retrieve it. "I'm assuming you're the girl from the Gazette. Dana phoned and told me you were on your way."

"Oh, right." My cheeks heated. He'd flustered me. Of course they knew each other. The way these two looked, they were probably dating.

"Just let me put the weights away," he said, "and then we can go talk."

I looked at the selection of dumbbells around his feet, the lightest one probably forty pounds. Feeling stupid at my earlier retort, I didn't want to stand around, watching him.

"Let me give you a hand."

A laugh bubbled up from his throat, right up until the point I bent and picked up one of the weights, one handed. I lifted the dumbbell and stacked it back in the rack and turned to find him staring at me.

I stared back. "What?"

"You got some muscles hidden under there?"

I realized what I'd done.

"Yoga," I told him in a rush. "Builds up some amazing strength. Nothing like using your whole body as a weight."

Flynn studied me again with that intense stare. His eyes had the sort of clarity I'd expect to find in a glacial pool or in the sea of somewhere tropical and untouched.

He nodded, but his eyes were narrowed, as though he were agreeing with me but thinking something else. "Maybe I'll have to give it a go then."

I laughed, a high-pitched titter, and cringed at the sound. "You should," I said, hoping he wasn't going to ask me for lessons. Other than a brief fad last year doing Bikram yoga—where I'd been stuck in a room with thirty other people to sweat out fat and toxins—I didn't know anything about it.

He tilted his chin toward me. "Look, give me five minutes to shower and change, and I'll meet you outside. Then you can grill me."

"Sure."

I left the remainder of the weights where they were.

I sat at a picnic table set in the small courtyard in front of the gym. My hands rested on the table, and I absently picked at the dry skin around my nails. Weirdly, I was looking forward to being in Flynn's presence again. While the jock persona did nothing for me, something about him had sparked my interest. At least he hadn't attempted to shake my hand or touch me in any way, and for that I was grateful. Normally, I avoided contact with other people, but today's multiple introductions had left me open.

I lifted my head to find Flynn striding across the courtyard toward me. His hair was still damp from the shower, making it a shade darker. With his hair being so short, I was sure it would have the texture of velvet if I ran my hand across his head. I shook the thought away; I'd just been relieved that he'd made no attempt to touch me, I certainly shouldn't be thinking about touching him.

"Hey," he said as he slid onto the bench opposite me. "I just realized you never told me your name."

"Elizabeth." I was certain the extended hand would come and I'd see something I didn't want to. Miraculously, it didn't.

"Elizabeth…" He seemed to mull it over. "Pretty."

"Thanks." I tilted my head. "I bet you say that to all the girls."

"Only the ones who have pretty names."

I cocked my eyebrows. "Puh… lease. Anyway, everyone calls me Beth."

He grinned and folded his arms on the table. "Sorry, can't help myself. So how come you're here interviewing me, Beth? Shouldn't you be hanging out with other freshers and getting settled in?"

"I'm not really into the socializing thing. I prefer work."

"You know what they say about all work …?"

"Are you able to say anything that isn't a cliché?"

He held his hands up in surrender and laughed, a full-belly laugh that made me want to laugh with him. "Okay, okay. I was just messing with you. So if you're so focused on your studies, don't you think you should ask me some questions?"

"Actually, I should probably be honest. I'm not even sure what I'm supposed to ask you. I don't know anything about the swim team."

He ran a hand across the top of his drying head. "That's Dana for you. She likes to throw people in at the deep end, see what sort of stuff they're made of."

"See if they sink or swim?" I said.

He laughed again. "Now who's talking in clichés?"

I grinned and went back to picking the skin on my nails. I looked back up at him. "So you guys know each other well?"

"We're both from Sage Springs, so yeah, I guess you could say that."

"*Really* well?" I probed.

His head jerked back, his eyebrows knitting in the middle. "Oh, man, no. She's more like the big sister I never wanted."

"Oh, she's older than you then?" I remembered the glimpse I'd gotten from her as she shook my hand, that of the older man with the salt and pepper hair. I didn't normally see anything too far ahead—months or days as opposed to years, so perhaps I should have been more aware that Flynn wouldn't be Dana's type either.

"Yeah, she's in her final year."

"And you're…?"

"In my second," he said slowly, as if I should have already either known or figured it out. Okay, that made him nineteen. Not quite so intimidating. I felt like I'd asked far too many questions around his personal life. If I didn't switch the topic, he was going to get the wrong idea.

I fished in my bag and pulled out my hardback notepad and pen.

Flynn filled me in on everything happening with the swim team—upcoming races and training schedules. I diligently scribbled down all the information he fed me, while sneaking glances at his face. He seemed to come alive when he spoke of his time in the pool, of lap-times and formations. His hands spoke for him, gesturing to highlight some particular fast time or stroke.

Just as I was writing down his final thought about which other college teams were the ones to beat, his hands dropped to the table. He folded his arms in front of him and leaned forward, his chest resting against well-muscled forearms.

"So tell me about you, Beth. What brings you to Sage Springs?"

His direct question caught me off guard, and I glanced up from my notebook.

"Errr… college?"

"Yeah, I think I figured that one out for myself. I meant why Sage Springs? You don't strike me as a small town girl."

I cleared my throat. "I'm not. I'm from Los Angeles. West Hollywood, to be exact."

"Daughter of a film star?"

No, a vampire.

"Not quite." I looked down at my hands again, self-conscious, the heat rising in my face.

"Only child, though. I can tell."

Something about the comment jarred me, and my head snapped back up again. "What's that supposed to mean?"

He shrugged. "You just have that 'single-child' vibe."

"Why?"

He must have realized he'd pissed me off, because he sat back and raised both hands in a 'surrender' gesture. But I wasn't going to let him get away that easily.

"So what about you? I suppose you come from a family of six—after all, I'm guessing there isn't a whole lot else to do around here."

He flashed me a grin, showing off his straight white teeth and the dimple in his left cheek. "Nah, takes one to know one."

I felt my defensive posture relax, my shoulders sinking.

"Oh … Oh right. You're an only child as well."

"So I was right then?"

"Yeah. I guess you were."

I've never been comfortable with people asking about my background. The story I've told so many times about my dad's condition always felt false on my tongue. I'm a terrible liar.

I scooped up my notepad and pen and smiled brightly at him. "Well, I think I've got everything. Thanks so much for making things easy for me."

A trace of confusion rippled across his handsome features, but he didn't argue with me. "Okay, no problem." We both stood, and he held out his hand to me, the gesture I'd been trying to avoid this whole time. I hesitated, trying to figure out which would be worse, seeing something secret to him or being rude enough to ignore the handshake. A flash of inspiration hit me and I held out my pen.

"This is Dana's. If you see her, could you give it back?"

Again, I'd thrown him, but his fingers closed around the pen. "Uh, sure."

"Thanks so much. See you around, I guess."

"I guess."

I left him standing there, holding my pen. I walked away, trying to keep my pace even and not break into the run my legs seemed determined to do.

CHAPTER 5

I GOT BACK to my room to discover Brooke had made a couple of friends. The three girls sat on Brooke's bed, their heads together as they giggled and gossiped. They didn't even notice my entrance, and I sidled over to my side of the room, hoping things would stay that way.

They didn't.

Brooke spotted me. "Oh, hey." Then she turned back to her new friends, "This is my roommate, Beth."

The two girls each lifted a hand in a wave. "Kayla," introduced the dark-haired girl with the coffee colored skin.

"I'm Erin," added the other girl, a brunette, like me.

"We're going out tonight, if you wanna come." said Kayla. "Every year, a carnival comes to town right at the same time the new intake starts. It's kinda traditional for everyone to go down on the first night. You up for it?"

I wondered why Flynn hadn't mentioned something, but shrugged it off. He obviously had better things to do than hang around with a fresher. "Sure, sounds fun."

Brooke smiled, but it was what I'd started to think was her usual 'fake' smile. I had the feeling I didn't exactly fit in with what she was looking for, friend-wise. Both girls currently sitting on her bed wore immaculate makeup, complete with skinny jeans and strappy cami-tops. I'd change into jeans before that evening, but I'd have to make a judgment call on the length of my sleeves, something that had nothing to do with the temperature outside.

"Well, we'll be leaving in less than an hour," said Brooke. "So if you want to come, you should probably get ready."

My stomach twisted with a sickening sensation. I knew she was making a point about my scruffy appearance, that she didn't want to be seen with me looking like a street urchin. Part of me wanted to tell her to screw it, and that I'd go on my own, looking however I wanted. But the other part of me desperately wanted to fit in. I'd spent so much of my time in Los Angeles without a real social group to speak of. I didn't want to be an outsider here, too.

"No worries." I gave her a tight smile. "I was just going to take a shower now. I had a long drive, you know?"

One side of her mouth turned up in a smile, but it didn't reach her light blue eyes. "Okay. Later then." And she ducked her head back down to continue to gossip with her friends.

I gave a sigh and opened my bag to fish out my wash bag, towel, and a change of clothes. I headed down to the showers, hoping I'd find the place empty. I didn't want to risk bumping into anyone else when I was anything less than fully dressed.

My luck was in on this occasion. The bathroom was empty.

Quickly, I stripped off my sweats and stepped into one of the stalls. A fiddle with the faucet sent a gurgle up the pipes, and a moment later cold water drenched down on top of my head. I bit down on a shriek at the chill of the water and forced myself to stand beneath it until the temperature warmed up.

I soaped my hair and body, letting the water wash away the grime of my journey.

My fingers ran down the skin of my forearms. A couple of weeks had passed since the last time I'd lost control, and the scars that often littered my arms had practically disappeared. I figured I might get away with short sleeves after all. In the moonlight and dancing colored lights of the carnival, the remaining scars would be invisible.

I was relieved. I didn't want to feel like an outcast or a freak. More than anything, I wanted to fit in. While I knew I'd never slot into one of the popular girl crowds, I didn't want to attract glances for the wrong reasons.

Feeling clean and refreshed, I climbed out of the shower and dried myself off.

I tugged on my light blue jeans, the denim as soft as worn cotton. Over my head, I pulled a black, sleeveless tee, the sparkling mouth and tongue emblem of the old band *The Rolling Stones* blazed across the front. I caught my hair up into a high ponytail and secured it with a band. It only took me a moment to debate my choice of footwear. I didn't do heels, so it was either my biker-boots or sneakers. To go with the top, I went with the boots.

I still had half an hour to kill before the girls were heading to the carnival. Perhaps I was being a coward, but I didn't want to go and sit back in my room, trying to make small talk about clothes, makeup, and boys—things I wasn't interested in. Instead, I left my floor and headed down to ground level, pushing out of the doors and into fresh air. The sky had grown a dusky pink and purple as the sun slipped, unseen by me, beneath the horizon.

Pulling my cell phone from my bag, I checked it for messages from my mom. I wanted to wait until dusk before calling home, but because the time zone here was three hours ahead of L.A., I would need to wait until later that night. That way both parents would be available for me to speak to. It would hurt my dad's feelings if I called beforehand and only spoke to Mom, but right at that moment I would have given anything to hear a friendly voice.

With a sigh, I pocketed my phone and made my way back up to the room to see if Brooke and her friends were ready.

WE APPROACHED THE carnival, the entrance marked by a huge, metal archway, with 'welcome' written across it in tall, red and yellow letters. The midway was alive with music and lights. Stalls selling all types of foods—funnel cake, caramel apples, French fries, and hot dogs—were spliced with stands with games such as the Crossbow Shoot, Water Guns, and Balloon and Darts. Stuffed animals hung in clear plastic bags, and more prizes lined every shelf. The big rides such as the Chair-O-Planes, Zipper-ride and Ferris wheel created the biggest attractions, marks queuing to get on. People buzzed around everywhere, the sweet scent of cotton candy and the irresistible tang of frying onions filled the air.

"Oh, boy, hottie alert," said Kayla, nudging me in the side.

I looked over at her, and she nodded in the direction of a group of guys hanging out around the back of the Tilt-a-Whirl.

"You know who that is, don't you?" said Brooke. "That's Flynn Matthews. He's something of a rising star around here."

"He can rise around me anytime," said Kayla, her eyebrows shooting up her forehead, eliciting a squeal of delight from Erin.

Brooke shook her head. "Nah, he's all about sport. He's not interested in mucking around with girls. I heard he had a serious girlfriend last year, but she broke his heart and messed up his whole training schedule. It nearly ruined his career, so he's stayed away from the dating scene since then." She sighed, her shoulders sagging. "Shame. He's just my type."

Kayla laughed. "He's everyone's type!"

I was listening to this new information and simultaneously watching Flynn laugh and talk with his friends out of the corner of my eye. I certainly hadn't taken him for someone who was willingly abstaining. Not that I was interested. Even if I was attracted to a guy, I couldn't imagine how it would work with me being able to catch glimpses of his past or future. What if I saw him cheating on me in the future? Would I end things based on a crime he hadn't even committed yet, or would I have to wait it out, knowing what he was going to do, but unable to act on it until I caught him in the act?

Lost in my own thoughts, I'd not realized I'd been staring. One of Flynn's friends—a shorter guy with light brown hair—punched Flynn in the arm, and Flynn jumped away from him, laughing. The movement changed his line of sight, and he caught me watching him. A wide smile spread across his face, and he said something to his group and then started walking over.

Kayla's mouth dropped open. "Holy crap. He's coming over."

Brooke shot me a confused look, but she didn't have time to say anything. I couldn't help the slight feeling of smugness that came over me at the sight of the expression on her face. She looked as though she wondered if she'd misjudged me.

"Hey, Beth," Flynn said, flashing that wide, dimpled grin. His eyes cast over my companions. "Hi, ladies. You enjoying the carnival?"

"We've only just got here," I said, the sudden compulsion to hustle everyone away from him casting over me. "We haven't even had a chance to look around yet."

Brooke stepped forward and swung her sheet of blonde hair behind her shoulder before holding out a hand to him. "Hi, I'm Brooke."

He smiled at her and took her hand. "Flynn," he said. I tried not to get a flash of jealousy. I had nothing to be jealous about.

"I know who you are." She flashed her billion-watt smile, and I tried not to cringe. "You're something of a star around these parts."

"Oh, you're local then?" His forehead creased. "I don't recognize you."

She issued a small titter of laughter. "Oh, I'm from Sage Springs, but I've been away a lot. You'd probably know of my family—the Squires? They own half the land around here."

He lifted his chin, his aqua-green eyes narrowing slightly. "Oh, right." He turned his attention back to me, shifting his body slightly so he angled Brooke out of the conversation. "You want to go on any of the rides, Beth? My treat."

I lifted my hands in defense. "Oh no. I'm not good with rides. I don't like heights, and I really suffer from motion sickness."

The other girls were staring at me like I was insane, their eyes burning into me. I did my best not to make eye contact with any of them. I think if Flynn had offered to take any of them to do anything—naked bungee-jumping, diving with sharks, wing-walking—they'd probably have jumped at the chance. I can't say I wasn't tempted, if only to give Brooke a poke in the eye, but I didn't want to give Flynn the wrong idea. While I was sure he was only being friendly, there was just enough tension between us to make me wonder if there was something more than a friendly offer in his words.

His shoulders fell, but he gave a shrug. "No worries. Maybe we can do something a little more …" he searched for the right word. "Immobile next time."

I laughed. "Sure."

Flynn stuffed his hands in his jeans pockets. "Later, ladies." And he turned and walked back to his group, who'd been watching.

As soon as he reached a safe distance, Kayla jabbed me in the ribs again, this time hard enough to hurt. "Okay, spill it. How the hell do you know him?"

"We just got talking." Not wanting to ruin my sudden allure of 'cool,' I added, "In the gym."

Brooke looked me up and down, and gave a slow nod of understanding. I realized she'd just pieced my sweat outfit of earlier with my assumed workouts in the gym. She was way off course, but I wasn't going to correct her.

We continued to walk down the midway, rides bordering us on both sides. Screams heightened with a combination of fear and elation filled the air. Different pop songs, fighting to be heard, blasted from numerous loudspeakers, fading away from one ride and strengthening at another.

A stand with hundreds of bags of pink cotton candy caught my attention. The treat was my mom's favorite, and the sight and smell of the spun sugar evoked a memory of home. A sudden pang of homesickness stabbed me. My mom would always buy me some if we ever went to a carnival or pier together.

"Hang on a sec, guys," I called out to the others. I hadn't bothered to bring my purse, but I'd stuffed a couple of bills in the back pocket of my jeans. I waited in line, and when I reached the counter, ordered a bag.

I returned to the girls, the bag already open and the sweet hit of sugar on my tongue.

Brooke arched her eyebrows. "That will turn straight into fat, you know?"

I grinned. "And it's worth every calorie."

We started to walk again, and I people watched, taking in all the different groups, trying to figure out which, like me, were new in town.

As I looked over, something—or someone—stole my breath.

CHAPTER 6

THE YOUNG MAN stood, balanced on the edge of the Waltzer, giving each car an extra shove as it passed. The girls inside the cars squealed with laughter, while the guys they were with bit down on their yells, trying to remain cool.

He wasn't particularly tall and didn't possess the broad-shouldered physique of Flynn, but he had high cheekbones and a full mouth, combined with a square jaw. A dramatic combination of feminine and masculine features.

Something about the sight of him made me stop short, my new friends continuing to walk on without me. As I stood, staring, he turned his head and caught my eye. Immediately my heart raced, my stomach lurching into my throat. His bright blue gaze eyed me curiously, and he pushed a hand through his jaw-length, black hair. I forced myself to look away. Heat flooded my cheeks, and I stared at the dirt ground, my cotton candy all but forgotten.

My heart pounded a tribal beat in my chest, my breath quickened. I forced myself to lift my head, my eyes automatically searching him out again.

Despite being with their boyfriends, I didn't miss how most of the girls threw glances in his direction, giving extra screams and head tosses whenever their turn came for him to push their cars. He looked to be around our age, perhaps slightly older, but he obviously didn't go to our school. He had the self-assured air of someone who knew where he belonged, even if where he belonged was constantly on the move. The dark stranger was obviously one of the carnival crowd.

Look at me again, I willed. *Notice me.*

I'd never learned if persuasion was part of the gifts I'd been cursed with due to my part-vampire gene pool, but this time it seemed to work. He gave another car a shove and then lifted his head and stared right at me.

One side of his full lips turned up in a lop-sided grin, and he gave me a slow, but definite, nod.

Flustered, I didn't even return the smile, but instead looked away and quickly started walking again, trying to catch up with the other girls, who hadn't even noticed I'd stopped. My heart still ran in a pitter-patter, hard enough that it seemed to be beating against my ribs, and heat still burned my cheeks.

As I walked, I glanced to my right. He was no longer looking at me, concentrating instead on his job. A gypsy? Was that what he was? Someone who traveled with the carnival?

Suddenly, a strange buzzing sounded in my ears, as though I were suffering from tinnitus after going to a rock concert. The music seemed to slow down, sounding like morphed voices on an old record player. Everything felt distant, and the world seemed to drag around me, the spinning machines now creeping on slow-down. The edges of my vision blurred, but the center of my line of sight sharpened and focused. My gaze was drawn, dragged into a certain spot at the base of the Waltzer, not far from where the dark haired guy was still standing.

I gripped my fists to my sides, but I could neither turn away, nor walk toward the thing that had gripped my attention. I zoned in on a particular spot, the area racing into my vision as though I'd pressed the zoom button on my camera. Metal plates vibrated under the force of the whizzing cars. As I stared, a part of the plate began to move more than the rest, the vibrating turning to actual shaking. A screw popped out of its holding, quickly followed by the one beside it.

Still frozen in one spot, I couldn't move. In slow motion, one of the cars hit the loose spot, and the whole plate came free. The air was filled with the sound of screams as the plate wrenched away under the force of the movement. Like I was watching a slow-motion car accident on a movie, the car spun off the ride and into the people standing around. A screech of metal on metal filled my ears, cutting right through me. The terrified screams of the bystanders drowned out everything else.

I gasped and squeezed my eyes shut. As soon as I did, my hearing went back to normal, my ears popping as though I was on a descending aircraft.

The sounds of the carnival—music, laughter, bells ringing—met my ears. Not the screams of terror I had been expecting. I opened my eyes to find everything was back to normal. No signs of anyone hurt. But I couldn't change what I had seen. Something was wrong with the ride, and I didn't know if the accident would happen mere minutes from now, or possibly months, but I had to do something.

My bag of cotton candy fell to the ground and bounced once before coming to a rest. I broke into a sprint and pushed my way between the small crowds of people—fellow student-types, families, even an elderly couple watching the fun—and jumped up onto the edge of the ride where the leather-jacketed guy was standing.

"Hey!" I had to yell to be heard over the music, which was almost painfully loud. "You need to stop the ride."

He turned to face me, both confusion and recognition passing across his face. "What?"

"Cut the power. Now! There's going to be an accident."

Despite my panic, in the back of my mind I was vaguely aware that launching myself onto the ride, and yelling at the cute guy running it, made me look like the one thing I always tried so hard not to be, a freak. In the crowds, people were exchanging glances, and though I couldn't hear what they said to each other over the music, I knew they were questioning my sanity. But they couldn't stay where they were. The small crowd was standing in the exact place the runaway car would land.

"Get out of the way!" I yelled at them, sweeping my arm to the right as though trying to herd them. "It's dangerous. Move out of the way."

I caught sight of Flynn's blond head and the concerned expression on his face, and my heart sank.

A hand caught my arm, and the carnival boy dragged me back around to face him.

"What the hell are you doing? Are you crazy or something?"

Sum-ting. Even over the music, I detected the faint Irish lilt in his voice.

"One of the plates is loose. You've got to stop the ride or there is going to be an accident."

"What are you talking about?" He had to shout to be heard and leaned in closer to me. I tried not to tremble at having him in such close proximity. "How could you know that?"

"I… I saw something. A screw came out from beneath one of the cars. It's not safe!"

Something in my expression must have registered with him. Instead of getting me hauled off by security or the cops, he frowned at the plates of the ride.

He reached out and touched my arm. "Wait here."

My whole arm fired with goose bumps, and I stared at his leather clad back as he leaped deftly between the spinning cars and to the center of the ride where an older, fat man sat in a booth.

I didn't see anything, I realized.

His touch on my arm hadn't caused any images to flash in my head. That had been the second time today I'd not seen something about a person when they'd touched me.

The strange buzzing pierced my head again, and I clamped my hands to my ears. My eyes darted frantically at the spot where I'd seen the screws come loose, but the cars flew by making it impossible for me to see anything.

The accident I'd witnessed, if only in my head, wasn't going to happen weeks or even days from now. It was going to happen any minute.

"Do it!" I yelled at the booth. "Shut the power down now!"

The ride powered down at the exact moment the car rattled loose. Screams issued around the crowd as the car spun off the track, but at nothing like the extreme speed I had witnessed. Even so, it flipped as it careened off the ride, scattering the crowd, sending people running. The car behind followed, but at a much slower velocity so it came to a standstill half on and half off the platform.

I bolted from the ride and down into the crowd, heading to the overturned car. The muffled cries of fear and possibly even pain came from the couple trapped inside. I was strong enough to flip the Waltzer car, but I couldn't risk doing so in front of crowds of people. All I needed was a couple of others to make it appear as though the righting of the car wasn't all down to me.

"Help me!" I cried.

A few of the guys ran forward to help.

Myself, the carnival guy, Flynn, and the friend I'd seen thumping Flynn, all lined up on one side. Together we heaved. The car felt light to me, but the men on either side of me strained, so I forced myself to hold back, though doing so pulled my emotions two ways. I didn't want to leave these people trapped any longer than needed, knowing they could be badly hurt. I couldn't smell blood, but I needed to protect myself.

Together, we turned the car over, righting the terrified couple still strapped inside. The girl must have hit her head, as a lump like a golf ball was starting to protrude over her left eyebrow. The boy clutched at his shoulder, wincing in pain. Both were pale-faced and shaking.

Mutterings came from the crowd, a few people nodding or pointing toward me, discussing my foresight of the accident. The crazy reaction I'd had right before the ride broke loose hadn't gone unnoticed.

Before anyone could accost me and start pelting me with questions, I ducked my head down and shoved my hands in my jean pockets, trying to make myself smaller, less noticeable. I took off, slinking between the rides, planning to put a good distance between myself and the midway.

A male voice with an Irish lilt called to me, but I continued to walk away.

"Hey! Are you all right?"

I didn't answer him. Instead, I picked up my pace.

His footsteps turned into a jog, and he caught me by my arm, pulling me back around to face him.

"Wait up!"

The sight of him took my breath away, like he'd literally punched me in the chest and winded me. The Cupid's bow, the full lower lip. The sharp cheekbones, and the dark shadow across his jaw. His eyes were an incredible shade of dark blue, especially in the moonlight, cast beneath thick, dark brows which were drawn down in concern. He was the most beautiful thing I had ever seen.

"What's the story?" he asked, his eyes studying my face. "How the hell did you know what was going to happen?"

"I didn't." I pouted my lower lip like a sulky child.

His heavy, dark eyebrows lifted. "Uh, yeah, you did. You shouted at me to stop the ride."

I looked away, studying a chip packet someone had carelessly littered. "I told you, I saw a screw come loose."

"At the speed the ride was going? In the dark?" He couldn't hide the disbelief in his voice.

"Yeah. Let's just say I have good eyesight."

I looked down at where his hand was still wrapped around my forearm.

A red haze descended upon my vision and a beating filled my head—*thu-thump, thu-thump, thu-thump.* My mouth sapped dry of moisture, and a pain speared tight in my throat. I struggled to swallow. My heart rate stepped up a notch.

Oh crap.

CHAPTER 7

I YANKED MYSELF out of his grip, tears blurring my vision. It was happening again, the thing I'd tried so hard to deny to myself.

The person people saw on the outside wasn't the same as the person who lurked within the slightly scruffy, try-too-hard exterior. I had darkness inside me. Writhing, coiling, scary darkness. I had been fighting it my whole life, but recently the darkness felt so much closer to the surface. My jaw ached, my throat running so dry I could barely swallow.

No, no, no, no. I closed my eyes, trying to focus in on my reaction, trying to will it away. I wanted to tell the boy standing in front of me to run, to get away, but the words wouldn't come out of my mouth.

Movement and a yell, not one caused by me, made my eyes ping open, the driving darkness at my soul retreating at the distraction.

"Leave her alone!"

Flynn stood between me and the new guy, his broad shoulders completely blocking my view of the dark hair and brooding eyes.

"You don't frighten me, jock-boy," the carny said. "And I was only talking to the girl."

"I don't want you even looking at her, never mind talking to her. Your kind is dangerous."

"Ay, don't I know it? Maybe you should think about that next time you take one of my kind on."

I moved around the side in time to see the dark haired boy start to push up the sleeves of his leather jacket.

"Hey! Quit it, both of you! I don't even know what you're fighting about."

Flynn looked to me. "He was bothering you, Beth."

"So what if he was?" I said, suddenly angered for a different reason. "Since when has it been your business to protect me? We barely know each other!"

"Exactly. This is none of your business," the carny guy said, picking up on my words.

I turned to him. "And I told you to leave me the hell alone. You don't want to get on my bad side, or being confronted by a six foot something jock will be the least of your worries."

"Ouch. You're a spiky one."

I could see him repressing a smirk, which only served to make me angrier. The aching in my jaw increased, my throat tightening. Both men were watching me, Flynn with a confused, hurt expression on his face, the carny guy with an amused smirk. I didn't even know his name, I realized.

I don't want to know his name, I tried to convince myself. But I did. Even with an annoying smirk that I wanted to slap off his striking face, I longed to know his name with every fiber of my soul.

But right now, the darkness was creeping over me. I was seeing red, literally. The veins on both of the men's throats, the spreading network across their inner wrists, all shone like a beacon to me. Threads of glowing red rivers of blood.

"Just leave me alone!" I finished, needing to get away from them both.

I turned and started to run, leaving the sounds and smells of the carnival behind me.

"Someone's going to want to talk to you," the carny boy shouted after me. "They're going to want to know what really happened."

I couldn't worry about that now. My mind was filled with the sound of blood pulsing through veins, my jaw now in serious pain. I needed to distract myself, to break the cycle. This had happened before, and only knowing I could stop it convinced me that I was safe to live among regular people. My plan had also consisted of avoiding all confrontation and intimate situations. Considering I'd only arrived today, I didn't think I'd done a particularly good job of that side of things.

I kept running until I was back on campus, and then took the stairs two at a time. I was out of breath, but not completely exhausted—my vampire genetics gave me stamina on top of everything else. I focused on one thing, stopping the frightening ache inside of me, the need and desire I'd only ever given into once as a child. I'd sworn to myself that I'd never be weak enough to give in again. I was well aware that succumbing to any blood lust would only make my vampire half stronger. I'd left Los Angeles to try to escape that part of me.

Heading straight to my room, I grabbed my wash bag. I'd hidden something in its lining, something I knew people would question if it was found. I'd agonized about whether or not to bring it, but now I was here and in this position, I was glad I had.

Most of the residents were still out, probably speculating about what had happened at the carnival, hanging out on the beach with a bonfire and a bottle of something alcoholic. I experienced a pang of envy for their easy lifestyles. Getting loose on a couple of drinks and making out with some hot guy they'd only just met. Alcohol had hardly any effect on my system, and making out with anyone was not going to happen because of my unfortunate habit of seeing into their lives and futures.

I took my wash bag into the bathroom, happy to have the place to myself. In haste, I scrabbled into my bag, slipping my fingers between the thin material and the padding, where I'd hidden the item I needed. I felt like a drug addict. I was getting my fix, in a way, even if it wasn't what I really needed. My fingers closed around the sliver of metal, and I pulled out the blade I'd taken from a smashed disposable razor.

Shaking, the red haze over my vision was making it hard for me to see. I could barely swallow, my throat felt as though I had swallowed a ball made up of the same blade I now clutched between my thumb and forefinger.

I didn't think any further. I lifted the blade and swiped it across the skin of my forearm, once, twice, three times. With each cut, the desperate need released me from its grasp, as though a man had stood with his hands around my throat, and had finally decided to let me go. The red haze swept from my vision, my mind clearing. I exhaled in relief.

The bathroom door swung open.

The movement made me jump, and I quickly cupped the sliver of razor blade in my palm and turned my body away, hiding my rapidly healing arm. My heart sank when I realized the person who'd joined me was also my roommate.

"Oh, God!" Brooke's small nose wrinkled in disgust, her eyes wide with horror. "What the hell are you doing?"

"Nothing," I said, quickly. The anger and bloodlust had already begun to ebb away, released with the cutting of my flesh and the beading blood. I couldn't explain why it worked, only that the action of cutting seemed to release something inside me. Perhaps it was like in history where doctors would cut people suspected of being possessed to let out the demon. Maybe that's what the self-harm was about—I was exorcising my own demons.

But Brooke wasn't going to be fobbed off with 'nothing.' Three strides brought her across the bathroom and she grabbed my shoulder, yanking me around. I put my arm behind my back, hiding what were now three shrinking wounds, but within a few hours would become no more than ridged scars. The action caused the razor blade to slip from my grasp and it fell to the tiled floor with a clink.

We both looked down. There was no hiding the thick ridge of blood now creating an almost black crust across the silver metal.

"Jeez." She made no attempt to hide the expression of disgust on her face. "What are you, some kind of Emo freak? Don't you think you should try a little more black eyeliner if you want to get into that crowd?"

"Get lost, Brooke," I snapped. I wanted her gone. Her insensitivity riled me.

"No way. You're my roommate. I deserve to know what I'm living with."

"What you're living with?" I couldn't believe the nerve of her. How did my actions affect her in any way?

"Yeah." She glared at me. "Someone prone to violence."

"Violence?" Okay, part of me knew she was close to the truth, but I'd never hurt anyone else. I'd only ever hurt myself. "I'm not violent."

"Then what do you call this?"

She reached around my body and yanked my arm forward for her to see. I breathed a sigh of relief. Blood still smeared my skin, but the cuts now appeared to be no more than a few scratches.

"I scratched it on some metal after the car came off the Waltzer," I said. "I thought I still had a splinter of metal in the cut. I was trying to get it out."

She narrowed her eyes. "With a razor blade?"

I shrugged. "I figured it was a bit like trying to get a splinter out with a needle. Didn't your mom ever do that to you?"

She released my arm. "My mom didn't ever do much with me."

I detected sadness in her voice, the way her gaze drifted away, as though looking toward her past.

Despite my angry thoughts only moments earlier, I wasn't one to hold a grudge.

"I'm sure she had her moments," I said gently, offering the other girl a smile.

But Brooke didn't return the emotion. Instead, she said, "What the hell do you know," and stormed from the bathroom, letting the door shut behind her with a bang.

Sighing, I bent to pick the blade from the floor. As much as I didn't want to admit it to myself, there was a good possibility I would need it in the future. I turned on the faucet and held the sliver of metal beneath the hot water, washing off the remnants of blood.

I hoped Brooke had bought my story. I'd known from the moment we'd met that she and I wouldn't be best buddies at any point, but I still wanted things to be amiable between us. The thought of dealing with tension every time I went to my room made me sick. All I wanted was an easy, normal life.

At least now the hour was late enough for me to call home. I had no intention of telling them what had happened that day. My mom would be on the first flight up here to drag me home.

Leaving the bathroom, I headed back outside to make the call. Several students loitered around, chatting to each other, or on their own cell phones, probably doing the exact same thing I was about to do. I felt sure I wasn't the only person missing home right now. Finding myself a secluded spot at the back of the building, I took my cell from my pocket. I didn't exactly have a lot of numbers programmed into my phone, so it only took a couple of seconds to get the phone ringing.

My mom answered on the first ring, and I smiled. I knew she'd be waiting by the phone.

"Elizabeth? Sweetie?"

"Hey, Mom."

"Hi, honey! I'm so glad you've called, finally. I've been worried sick all day."

"You could have picked up the phone and called me yourself."

"Oh, I didn't want to bother you. I knew you'd be settling in, meeting new friends. I didn't want to ruin your street-cred."

I cringed at my mother's choice of words. "Don't be silly. I did tell you'd I'd wait until Dad was up before I called."

"I know you did, but still ... I was worried you might have had a car accident or something."

I rolled my eyes. That was my mother—the constant worrier. I guess after everything we'd been through it was only to be expected. I'd almost died as a child, something they never spoke to me about and thought I couldn't remember, so it was only natural for her to be overprotective. Even so, her overprotective nature was definitely one of my reasons for wanting to get away from home. I loved her more than anything, but I needed my own space. I had no intention of telling her about the incident with the fallen wire on my drive into town, and that my car was in the shop.

"So you're okay, then?" she continued. "You've made some friends?"

"Yes," I said, thinking of Brooke and how I didn't think I'd ever be classed as a 'friend.' But then I remembered Flynn, Laurel, and even Dana. "I've made some friends," I told her. "Everyone has been great, and a group of us went out this evening."

I sensed her relax on the other end of the line. "That's wonderful, sweetie. Sounds like fun. I can't believe my baby-girl is all grown up and living away from home." She gave a sniff.

"I'm hardly a baby anymore, Mom."

"No, I know you're not. I'm just going to spend the next few months having to remember that you're not in the house anymore." She lowered her voice, though if my dad was anywhere in the vicinity he'd have heard her anyway. "The daytimes are going to be very lonely."

"So sleep in the day and spend time with Sebastian at night. Isn't that what you've been looking forward to all these years?"

She sighed. "I lose one of you, but gain the other. I just wish I could have both."

"You've still got me, Mom. I'm only at college."

I heard a muttered voice beyond my mother's. "Your father is hovering," she said. "I'd better pass you over."

"Sure, Mom. I love you."

"I love you too, sweetie. Stay safe."

There was a shuffling as she handed the phone to my father.

His deep voice came down the line, "Hey, kiddo." I pictured him standing in our hallway, with his pale skin and dark hair, still looking no more than mid-thirties, despite being hundreds of years old.

"Hi, Sebastian," I said with a grin, knowing my habit of using his first name irked him. "Sleep well?"

I felt the smile in the tone of his voice. "Like the dead. How are things with you? I assume by your mother's lack of panic that you made the rest of your trip safely."

I laughed. "Yeah, no twenty car pile-up on the freeway, or freak aircraft crashing into the school."

Just a freak electrical wire and a runaway carnival ride.

"Glad to hear it, though the way your mother has been acting, you'd think that's exactly what had happened."

"You've only been awake about ten minutes."

"Good thing, too. At least she only had herself to drive insane."

"You don't mean that."

It was his turn to laugh. "Of course not."

Despite his teasing, I didn't have any doubts that my father would always be there for my mom, Serenity. They'd been through so much together and regularly embarrassed me with their very public displays of affection. Okay, maybe not public, but certainly around the house, and that was enough for me. The last thing any kid wants to see is their parents making out on the couch.

"And how's everything else," Sebastian asked me. "How are you getting on with … things?"

I knew what he was asking me. Both my parents were aware of my precognitive abilities, though my mom liked to pretend I'd gotten a handle on everything. My dad, who had lived with his own abilities for hundreds of years and still struggled to fit in, understood a bit more.

"There have been a couple of weird moments, but nothing I can't handle."

No breathing came down the end of the line, I could have been speaking into a dead connection, but I knew I wasn't. "That's great. You know any time you need us, just shout and we'll be there."

"I don't need you coming to my rescue now, Dad. I'm a grownup. I want to handle things my own way."

"Too independent," he grumbled. "You always were."

"I think my genes have something to do with that." I paused. "Look, Dad, I really have to go. Some people are waiting for me."

"Okay, no problem, sweetheart, as long as we know you're okay. Shall I put your mom back on?"

"No, don't. You know what she's like, she won't let me go."

"Okay, we'll say bye to you together."

There was a muffled scrape and jointly their voices came down the line, "Bye sweetie, we love you!" I could picture them with their faces pressed close together as they both tried to use the phone simultaneously. The image made me feel strangely homesick, even though I'd been so desperate to escape all this time.

"I love you too, guys. I'll call soon, I promise."

I forced myself to hang up before the repetitions of 'I love you' came down the line.

As awkward as I felt heading back to our room, knowing Brooke would most likely be there, I had nowhere else to go.

I could always go and sleep in my rental car, but not only would it be super uncomfortable, I also didn't want to be a coward. Hiding from Brooke because she'd gotten an insight into my dirty little secret made me look pathetic.

I took a deep breath, forced my feet to move, and went back to our room. She was lying on her stomach, reading a book, and only glanced in my direction before turning back to it, a scowl narrowing her eyes.

I shrugged out of my jeans and undid my bra, slipping it out from beneath my top. I probably should have changed, but I only wore a camisole and panties to bed, and I didn't want to expose my skin to the other girl any more than I already had. Slipping beneath the bedcovers, I turned my back on Brooke, facing the wall. I pressed my face into the pillow I'd brought from home, wanting to be comforted by the feel and smells of home. Instead, the pillow only served to cause a huge wave of homesickness to rise up and crash over me.

Even though I had come to Sage Springs in order to escape the vampirism that had shadowed my entire life, right then I would have given anything to be at home with my mom and dad, Serenity and Sebastian.

CHAPTER 8

I STOOD ON a road on the outskirts of town. Pine forests bordered both sides of the road, but, beyond the bend ahead, I could just make out the lights of town glowing into the night sky.

A shiver wracked through me. What was I doing here? How did I even get here? The trees on either side of me rustled as a breeze stirred their branches. I needed to get out of the middle of the road, a car might come along any minute and mow me down, but at the same time I didn't want to go near the forest. I couldn't explain why, but something in my gut told me to stay away.

Movement on the road ahead caught my attention. A woman was walking up the road, a strange walk, her head held perfectly straight, staring ahead. She wore a long dress, though her feet were bare. I frowned. No, that was wrong. It wasn't a regular dress she wore, but a nightgown. Was the woman sleepwalking?

I began to walk toward her. "Hey, are you…?"

But I trailed off as someone else rounded the bend, appearing behind the woman. It was an older man this time. He wore only boxer shorts and an old t-shirt, but slippers were on his feet as he shuffled along.

What the hell?

More people appeared, a stream of them following the woman who'd come first. Couples, teenagers, even children, clutching their teddies, their hair mussed up as though they'd just gotten out of bed. All wore the same, blank expressions. All seemed to be coming from Sage Springs.

As I gawped at the spectacle, the first woman slipped off the road and between the trees, heading deeper into the forest.

"Hey, no!" I called out. "You don't want to go in there! Something bad is in the forest."

I knew it was true. Though I'd seen nothing to make me think such a thing, my instincts were rarely wrong.

A dream, I realized. I was dreaming one of those dreams. A dream that was trying to tell me something.

Though subconsciously I knew I was dreaming, I couldn't stop myself from reacting, from trying to change an event that wasn't even happening yet, if it was going to happen at all.

One by one, the people followed the woman, disappearing between the tree trunks, vanishing into the darkness. I ran to those who remained on the road, clutching at arms. "Don't go in there, please, don't follow her!" But no one listened. No one even appeared to notice me.

They could have been sleepwalking, but more than anything they just seemed… empty.

I WOKE THE next morning with absolutely no idea where I was. For a few wonderful, peaceful seconds, I'd completely forgotten about the events of the day before, but then they all came crashing down on me, and inwardly I shriveled.

Would someone, the police or people from the carnival, come and talk to me about my foresight of the accident? There was bound to be some kind of investigation, despite no one being seriously hurt.

Then I had Brooke to deal with.

I concentrated, but got no sense of anyone else in the room. No breathing or low thud of a heartbeat. Still facing the wall in the same position as I'd fallen asleep in, I cautiously rolled over to face the rest of the room. Brooke's bed was empty.

The absence of my roommate made me check the small alarm clock on my bedside table. Shit! I hadn't remembered to set it. It was almost eight thirty, and my class started at nine. I couldn't be late for my first class.

I grabbed my wash bag and a change of clothes, and raced to the bathroom for the world's fastest shower. I dried and dressed, dumped my stuff back in my room, and ran out of the building and toward campus. My first class was math—not my favorite—and I quickly checked the small map with my schedule, trying to locate the room I needed to be in. Luckily, I found it right before the bell went to mark the start of class, and burst through the door, flushed and with a sheen of sweat on my forehead. Most of the students were already seated, and I quickly scanned the room for a spare chair. My eyes met with a wide grin, and with a thrill I recognized the girl I'd met yesterday, Laurel, beckoning me over and motioning to the spare chair beside her.

I darted across the room, but someone else, a skinny guy wearing too-large jeans, tried to take the seat.

"Sorry, dude," Laurel said, reaching out to block him. "That seat's taken."

The boy cocked his eyebrows in disbelief, but didn't bother to argue, finding a different chair near the back of the room. I slid in beside Laurel.

"Thanks," I said. "I overslept."

"On your first day?" She had laughter behind her voice.

"I know, great start, huh? The thing is, I never oversleep!" Most of the time, I didn't need more than three or four hours' sleep a night. It was the reason I'd been able to make the drive up to Sage Springs in so little time. Yesterday's events had obviously taken their toll on me.

She leaned in, conspiratorial. "Dorm beds that comfy?"

I grinned. "I guess they must be."

A man walked into the room. He was handsome, in a clean cut kind of way, with salt and pepper around the edges of his dark hair, and creases at the corners of his eyes that looked to be more from laughter than age. I couldn't help myself. I stared at him, knowing my brow was creased in concentration, a couple of lines appearing between my own eyebrows.

"Settle down, everyone," he called out. "My name is Doctor Spencer, and I'm your math professor for your first year."

I recognized him, I knew I did, but I just couldn't place him.

"If you can open your text books at trigonometry..." Groans rose around the room. He laughed, "Come on, it's too early in the term for you to be jaded already."

He turned to his own book, a serious expression replacing the smile, and instantly I knew where I recognized him from. Dana's future. I quickly glanced around, wondering if I had missed her. But she wasn't in this class, of course she wasn't. She must be taking his class at a different time. Was that how they'd meet, I mused. Or did she already know him? She said her family was from around here, so their paths might have already crossed.

Doctor Spencer put us to work, talking us through the exciting world of lengths and angles of triangles. He was engaging and funny, not what I'd expect of a math teacher at all. He made the next hour pass quickly, despite the tedious subject, and eventually the bell rang and we were allowed to go.

I stood from my seat and gathered my belongings, heading out into the corridor.

Laurel fell in beside me. "So, did you hear about what happened at the carnival last night?"

I stiffened. "What do you mean?"

"There was an accident. One of the cars of the Waltzer came off the platform. People were inside, and it flew into the crowd. But apparently some girl seemed to know what was going to happen before it did."

"Really? No way." I mumbled, ducking my head down. "You weren't there though?"

"No, my family has a thing against the carnival people." Her lips twisted. "They can be a bit over protective." She must have realized something. "So you were there then?"

I felt my normally pale cheeks flush with color. "Yeah, I was there."

"But you didn't see anything?" She eyed me curiously.

I glanced away and mumbled, "No, I didn't."

Laurel either ignored my awkwardness or didn't notice. "What class have you got next?"

I was glad for the distraction. Checking my schedule, I said, "Looks like English Lit."

She grinned. "Great. Me too."

I wanted to feel pleased at our shared classes, remembering the hope I'd had at getting to know her the previous day, and also my lack of friends, but the mention of the carnival incident had set me on edge. The last thing I'd wanted to do was lie, but I couldn't stand the barrage of questions I knew would have followed.

A familiar blond head bobbed through the sea of students toward us. My gaze darted around, hunting for an escape route, but there was none. Flynn's eyes were locked directly on me.

"Hey, Beth," he said, coming to a stop directly in front of me, his large body blocking the way. "How're you doing? I've been worried about you."

"I thought I told you it wasn't your job to worry about me."

He shrugged. "Yeah, I know it's not my job, but that doesn't stop my brain from working. You seemed really upset last night, which I totally get, but then that carny guy was hassling you…"

I could feel Laurel watching the interaction with curiosity.

"I was fine. It was just a shock."

"You never explained how you predicted what happened."

Laurel butted in. "It was you? You're the one who warned everyone?"

The heat in my face increased. "I saw a screw pop out and roll to the ground, and the plate was coming loose."

"But you just said you didn't see anything?" Laurel said, confused.

"Sorry. I didn't want everyone to know."

I looked past Flynn's shoulder to see two police officers striding down the corridor toward us. "Oh, you've got to be kidding," I groaned. Was anyone going to give me a break today?

"Miss Bandores?" The male counterpart of the police duo asked, his eyes flicking between me and Laurel.

I lifted my hand as if answering in class. "Yeah, that's me."

"My name is Officer Logsdon," he said, then gestured to the woman at his side. "This is Officer Russo. Sorry to interrupt your first day, but I'm afraid we're going to need to ask you a few questions. Is there anywhere we can talk?"

Practically the entire school had stopped what they were doing, and now stood silently watching the interaction between me and the police officers. So much for keeping my head down and fitting in. I didn't know the campus well enough to know what rooms would be free, and I certainly didn't want to take them back to my room. Despite having an uncle in the police department (well, he was more a family friend than a real uncle), I still had an innate fear of authority. I was always certain I was doing something I shouldn't be, or would let something slip about what kind of creatures made up my family.

All I managed as a response was a shrug.

The officers exchanged a glance. "How about we talk in the patrol vehicle?" Officer Logsdon offered.

I shrugged again. "Sure."

The sea of students lurking in the hall to find out what was going on now parted like the Red Sea as the cops walked between them, followed by a sheepish me. I kept my head down, my long hair falling over my face, my stomach in knots. Most of these people probably didn't know what the police wanted with me, but I doubted it would stay that way for long. I understood how the gossip mill worked. Even if people didn't know what was going on, they'd probably make something up until they did.

I followed the officers out to the parking lot where my own rental car was parked. The cop car stood out like a beacon. The only thing getting more attention than the car was me. Officer Logsdon opened the back door of the patrol vehicle and I slipped into the back seat. Both officers climbed in the front and twisted back around to speak to me.

"I'm guessing you already know why we need to talk to you," the female officer, Russo, said.

I hazarded a guess. "The accident at the carnival last night?"

She nodded. "That's right. We had a number of people report that you predicted the accident about to happen and were actually trying to move people away from the ride only moments before the car spun off." She picked up her notes, "A Riley Draiodh said—"

I cut her off. "Who?"

"The young man working the ride. He says you seemed absolutely certain of what was about to happen. You told him the car was going to spin off into the crowd of people, something which happened only moments later."

I shrugged, while storing away the knowledge of his name for turning over later. *Riley Draiodh…*

"It was a lucky guess," I told her. "I saw a screw come loose and the car looked like it was lifting off the platform. Anyone else who noticed it would have assumed the same thing."

"But no one else did notice, did they? And there must have been fifty people standing around that ride."

"Are you trying to say I had something to do with it, and suddenly changed my mind and so warned everyone to get out of the way?" Despite my fear of authority, I couldn't help the sarcastic tone that entered my voice.

"Is that what happened?" Officer Logsdon said, not a trace of humor on his face.

"No, of course not! I only got here yesterday."

Officer Russo continued, "This is very serious, Miss Bandores. Several people were hurt in the incident, and the carnival has been shut down. If you know anything, I suggest you tell us now. It'll only look bad on you if we find out at a later date that you withheld information."

"I don't know anything else!"

My heart had fallen at the mention of the carnival closing. Did that mean the boy, Riley, would leave now? It seemed strange to think I might not see him again. I wasn't sure if it was one of my predictions, but I'd felt sure our paths would cross again.

The female officer checked her notes again, though I was certain she'd already planned exactly what she was going to ask me. "We also had an incident on Route Forty-Six yesterday afternoon in which you seem to have been involved."

I'd had to report the accident in order to claim on my insurance for damage to my car.

"Well, yes, but that had nothing to do with me. I just happened to be in the wrong place at the wrong time."

She studied my face and I shrank. "That happen to you often?"

I bristled. "Not normally. Must be something about this town."

She responded only with a "hmm," and scribbled something on her notepad.

"Anyway," I said. "Is it okay if I go now? My next class will start soon, and I don't want to be late quite so early in the term."

They exchanged a glance.

"All right," Officer Logsdon said. "If we need to ask you any more questions, I assume we can find you on campus."

"Yes, I'm staying in Caraway dorm."

Officer Russo leaned across the back of the seats and handed me a card. "If you hear anything or think of anything else, please give us a call."

My fingers closed around the card which contained her name and number. "Sure. No problem."

That seemed to be good enough for the moment. I climbed out of the car and tried to ignore all of the curious glances and whispers behind the backs of hands directed at me. I slouched further, trying to make myself as small as possible, wishing I could shrink enough for people not to notice me altogether. Sudden hot tears burned at the backs of my eyes, an overwhelming homesickness sweeping over me. Why had I bothered to come here? My parents had been right. I should have stayed close to home rather than trying to form a new life for myself. I could never escape what I was.

I slunk into my next class without even looking up to try to spot Laurel. I took a seat near the front and tried to concentrate as my new English Lit professor introduced herself and started to explain the course. Lifting the lid of my laptop, I did my best to hide behind it.

By the end of the lecture, my stomach was growling, signaling lunch time. I'd not had time to eat breakfast that morning and was starving. I didn't want to go into the dining hall, but I couldn't keep hiding.

You saved lives, I told myself. *You shouldn't be ashamed of what you did. You should be proud. So what if people are talking? They always talk. Give it another twenty-four hours and they'll be gossiping about some other poor soul.*

I wasn't a coward. I needed to be strong, and if that meant walking into the dining hall with my head held high, then that was exactly what I intended to do. I could hear my parents' voices in my head. *You're tough, you're strong. You've already been through more than any of these people could comprehend.*

I slipped my laptop into its case, and then put it in my bag, together with my text books. The bag was heavy, but I barely noticed as I slung it over my shoulder and headed out of the lecture hall to join the river of students. From my tour earlier in the year, I knew where the dining hall was located, so I headed there. The south dining hall was a new extension on the old building, with slanted glass panels as a roof which let in huge amounts of light. Round tables with comfortable padded seats were positioned around the middle of the large space. A number of leather couches were grouped together in one corner. The double doors were already propped open in expectation of the busy lunch period. Many of the tables already had students sitting at them. Most of the students who were relaxed and chatting easily with each other were older, second and third years. The few people lurking awkwardly around, trying to figure out which queue they were supposed to join, or with trays of food in their hands, wondering where to sit, were newbies like me.

There was a certain amount of comfort in knowing I wasn't the only one who felt out of place.

I joined the line for food, resolutely ignoring everyone else. I debated the salad bar, and decided after the day I'd already had that I deserved a burger and fries. I even added a chocolate milkshake to the mix. I'd probably have every other teenage girl in the room gasping in horror at my selection, but my half vampire genetics didn't allow me to put on weight. My weight had stayed exactly the same since I was fourteen. Besides, I wanted the comfort of some serious fat and carbs.

With relief, I spotted an empty table. Quickly, I crossed the dining hall and slid into one of the chairs, placing my tray on the table. I lifted my burger to my mouth, taking a huge bite, but I wasn't allowed any time to immerse myself in the comfort of processed food as someone sat down opposite me.

"You know that's not good for you?"

I lowered my burger to stare into his green eyes, and chewed and swallowed too fast. "What are you, Flynn? My substitute parent?"

He cocked an eyebrow. "Far from it, I'd hope. And I'd really hate to be your parent. Considering the cops turned up for you at school today, I think you'd drive them into an early grave."

I had to bite back a smile at the idea of my vampire father and vampire-blood taking mother meeting an early grave. "The cops only wanted to ask me a couple of questions," I told him, wiping grease off my chin.

He leaned forward. "And what did you tell them?"

"Exactly what I told you."

I refused to enlighten him about anything else. Though Flynn had so far seemed like a good guy, I didn't really know him. He might take whatever I told him and spread it around the gossip mill. I had a feeling enough people were talking about me already.

Another figure approached the table, and I glanced up to find Dana, the school's newspaper editor, standing there. She gave me a smile and slid into the seat next to Flynn.

"I hope you guys are finalizing the article I gave you to work on."

I glanced guiltily at Flynn. "Yeah, sure we are."

"Great, cause I need it by tomorrow to get it into the first print run."

I made myself smile back, though the last thing I'd thought about was the article. "Not a problem. I was just running over a couple of facts with Flynn."

Dana glanced to both sides of herself, and lowered her voice. "To be honest, Beth, I can't help wondering if I should take you off this report to work on something more interesting." She seemed to remember who she was sitting next to and glanced at Flynn. "Sorry, Flynn."

He shrugged his broad shoulders. "Not a problem."

"What do you mean?" I said, though I had a feeling I knew what was coming.

She leaned across the table, conspiratorial. "I hear you got a front row seat at last night's accident at the carnival?"

I shifted in my seat. I didn't want to lie to her. I had hoped to make the newspaper a bit of a home away from home, and, as lame as it seemed, I wanted Dana to like me. "Yeah, I guess you could say that."

"So how about you write me up a piece on what happened? You can tell everyone your point of view. It's the sort of thing that will make the front page."

She hadn't even seen any of my writing yet, apart from the few pieces I'd emailed her once I'd decided on which college I wanted to go to. This was a huge opportunity, but did I really want that much attention? Plus, this was a criminal investigation now. What would the police make of me plastering my story all over the front page of the school newspaper?

I said so to Dana and she screwed up her face in consideration. "You have a point. Let me check out what the law is in regards to you reporting the story, and I'll get back to you. But if it looks like there's no problem, will you do it?"

I couldn't see any other way around the situation. "Sure."

Dana began to get to her feet. She touched Flynn's shoulder. "You coming or staying?"

He glanced to me. "I thought I might hang out with Beth for a while."

Something about the tightness of her jaw and the hard glint in her blue-gray eyes at his words made me certain she hadn't really been asking him. "Are you sure about that?"

I'd been sure they weren't a couple before, but now I wasn't so certain. There was some kind of connection there, even if it wasn't romantic.

Flynn gave me an apologetic smile and got to his feet. The pair slunk away, shoulder to shoulder, Dana's red curls close to Flynn's buzzed blond head.

I turned my attention back to my burger. The meat had grown cold, the grease starting to congeal. I picked it up to take a bite, but changed my mind and set it back down, my nose wrinkled. I took a slurp of my milkshake instead and then absently chewed on a cold fry.

Whatever might be going on between them wasn't really any of my business, I decided. Of all people, I should be one who knew the value of other people's privacy. I'd lived for years wanting people back home to not ask questions about my own home life.

Whatever was going on between Flynn and Dana had nothing to do with me.

CHAPTER 9

THE AFTERNOON CLASSES passed by without event. I still felt eyes on me as I walked down the hall, and knew other students whispered behind their hands about me, but I did my best to ignore them. They would forget about me soon enough.

Wishing I had a room to myself, and praying Brooke would have found somewhere else to hang out for awhile, I headed back to my dorm.

Brooke wasn't in, but someone else was.

My eyes widened in shock, and I glanced back toward the door, wondering if I'd imagined things or had walked into the wrong room. But when I looked back, there he was, all dark, tousled hair and piercing blue eyes, sitting on my bed. The shock of seeing him was like someone had punched me in the stomach, not only because of the strangeness of finding a boy in my room, but because the sheer beauty of him left me breathless.

I fought against my body's reaction in order to get my brain to function again, and force my mouth to come out with a normal reaction to finding someone who was practically a stranger sitting on my bed.

"What the hell are you doing in my room?"

The window behind him was open, the wind causing the drapes to lift as though someone was behind them. I frowned. Had the weather suddenly changed? I didn't remember it being breezy when I'd crossed campus.

"And how did you get in here?" I continued, trying not to be distracted by his mouth. A crease ran vertically down the middle of his lower lip, the effect pouty and almost feminine. I bit my own lip in reaction, feeling the blood rush to the area, as I imagined my teeth biting down on his mouth.

I shook the thought from my head and focused on the important thing. The door had been unlocked. Had I forgotten to lock it, or had Brooke? But that still didn't explain how he'd made it through the front door without anyone challenging him.

One corner of that full mouth turned up. His blue eyes twinkled. "I sneaked in. I'm good at going unnoticed."

His Irish accent made my insides melt, but I forced myself to be hard. I wasn't one of those girls who turned into goo the moment they were in the presence of a hot guy.

"Not by me, you're not. Seems to me like you're everywhere I look. Now get out of here before my roommate gets back. She thinks I'm crazy as it is. You being here will make things even worse."

He got to his feet, but instead of walking out the door, he approached me. His eyes slightly narrowed, but didn't leave my face for a moment. My heart increased its pace with every step he took closer to me, my breath growing shallow.

He stopped a mere six inches from me, looking down at me so his jaw length hair fell around his face.

"Don't pretend having me in your bedroom does nothing to you."

I didn't want him to know he was right. I stepped back, trying to break whatever spell he had me under. "You leave me cold," I said.

Infuriatingly, he laughed. "See, I knew you were icy. Maybe that's what I should call you from now on, Icy."

"You don't need to call me anything," I shot back.

"Aww, come on, Icy. You don't really want me to leave."

I didn't. He was driving me nuts, but I certainly didn't want him to go. He'd occupied my thoughts constantly since I'd first seen him working the ride. But at the same time, I was terrified of Brooke coming back and what her reaction would be. The girl already had it in for me. But yet I couldn't stand not knowing the reason for Riley being in my bedroom.

"Okay, Riley," I submitted. "Tell me what you want and then get the hell out of here."

He jerked back in surprise. "How do you know my name?"

I knew this would throw him. "The cops told me."

"They came to speak with you already?"

"Sure did. Were asking me lots of questions about you, how I knew you, what kind of set up you had going on."

I enjoyed the falter in his cocky attitude.

"And what did you tell them?"

"I don't see why I need to tell you anything. As far as I can see, you owe me. If I'd not warned all those people about the ride, you and the rest of your crew could be up for a manslaughter charge right now."

"So come on, straight up with me. How did you know the accident was about to happen?" He eyed me, no longer quite so predatorial, but more curious. He knew there was something different about me, he just had no idea what—or at least I hoped he had no idea what.

"There's nothing more I can tell you. Sorry."

"Listen. If you won't tell me anything more, you need to watch yourself. You've gotten yourself noticed a couple of times now by the guys who run the carnival, and they don't like what they don't understand."

I lifted my eyebrows. "Watch myself? Are you threatening me?"

"No, I'm warning you." He sounded exasperated.

"Warning me or threatening me, they both sound the same. You're telling me that unless I tell you exactly what happened, your guys are going to come after me."

He shrugged, but had the decency to look uncomfortable for the first time. "I'm only telling you the truth."

"Yeah, well, your truth sucks. Now get the hell out of my room before I scream, and really give you something to worry about."

"Fine, but don't say I didn't warn you." Riley walked to the door, opened it, peered one way and then the other. He offered me a wink, and slipped from the room.

I sat on the edge of my bed, shaking. How could one boy create such a mixture of emotions inside me? Part of me wanted to hit him, while the other just wanted to be near him. There was no denying there was something magnetic about Riley. He might have decided there was something different about me, but I couldn't help feeling I was missing something about him, too.

Did I really need to be worried about the men from the carnival coming after me? After all, I didn't do anything wrong. Surely it was just an accident.

Something occurred to me.

Unless it wasn't an accident. Unless something else was supposed to have happened, and I interfered, or else the *accident* was supposed to have happened, but the fact someone seemed to know about it spooked them?

The door burst open again, and I shot upright, my nerves jangling. Was he back? But instead of a cocky dark-haired gypsy boy, a gaggle of girls walked in, all laughing and talking, their heads together. I never felt like more of an outsider than when I was in this situation. No matter how hard I tried, I couldn't fit in with these perfect images of the all-American college girl. My soul was too dark.

"Hey, Beth," one of the girls, Kayla, said with a bright smile. "How were your first classes? I think I saw you in bio. I tried to catch your eye, but you were so focused on your laptop, I couldn't."

"Oh, yeah," I said, forcing a smile. "Catching up on my email, you know?"

"Oh, sure. I know exactly what you mean. I always struggle to pay attention when I have mail."

Brooke had entered with them, but she barely looked at me. I had to assume from the fact the other girls were speaking to me like I was a normal human being that Brooke hadn't told them about the incident in the bathroom. For that, at least, I was grateful.

Brooke's other friend, Erin, sat down on my bed and grinned at me, bright-eyed. "So spill the gossip!"

Unease swept through me in a wave. "What gossip?"

"You know, about what happened last night."

My eyes flicked to Brooke, but she gave a slight shake of her head. Okay, so she hadn't told them. Maybe she wasn't as bad as I first thought. Of course, they meant the carnival.

Erin flicked her curls from her face. "I heard the cops were on campus today looking for you."

I shrugged to try to show them how unbothered I was by all of this. "They found me. They just wanted to ask me a couple of questions."

Kayla plonked herself down on the other side of me, leaving Brooke standing on the other side of the room. She smiled, as if joining in with the group, but I could sense the cold stare in her eyes. I realized that my escapades at the carnival last night had made me a bit of a celebrity, and the arrival of the police had only compounded the idea that I was some kind of bad-ass. I guessed that despite the whispers, this made me stand out, and everyone wanted the inside news on what had happened. Of course, it now felt as though I was stealing Brooke's friends from her, and I wondered how long she would hold onto the secret about what she'd caught me doing last night.

I told myself my self-harm was different to what some other teenage girls put themselves through. After all, I healed almost as quickly as I cut, and I wasn't cutting in order to release whatever pent up, teenage emotions I was going through. At least, I told myself that wasn't the reason I did it. But perhaps my reaction to other people's extreme emotions by wanting to bite them was my own strange, half-vampire, teenage body's reaction. Other teenagers might be controlled by their hormones. I was controlled by my part-vampire genetics.

But no, they didn't control me. I had a handle on it. Or I hoped I did.

"So are you coming to the social tonight?" Kayla asked me. "We're all planning to go if you want to come with?" She looked over to Brooke. "That's okay, isn't it?"

Brooke shrugged, but didn't look at me. "Whatever."

I wondered if Laurel would be going. I hadn't spoken to her since the police carted me off in the hall, and we hadn't bothered exchanging numbers. Fingers crossed, she would be there. I could do with a cheerful face whose company I could relax in.

I just hoped that after I'd been caught out in my blatant lie that she'd still want to talk to me.

CHAPTER 10

MUSIC BLASTED FROM the sports hall, banners strung out front welcoming the new influx of students. Small clusters of students hung out on the grass outside, chatting to each other. A group of guys threw a football around and yelled at one another, distracted only by the girls walking around in heels and short skirts.

Despite the balmy evening, I'd opted for a long sleeve top in floaty chiffon, and another pair of jeans. I needed to keep my arms covered because, while the cuts from the previous night were now scars, they were still visible. I never felt comfortable showing off my legs.

The three girls walking with me didn't have any of my inhibitions. Brooke wore a skin-tight short dress, while Kayla rocked a pair of low slung skinny-fit jeans with a top that exposed her stomach, and Erin sported a strappy cami that left little to the imagination, and a flippy, short skirt. I felt like a total frump walking beside them. The only benefit

I could think of was that at least I didn't need to worry about any of the guys checking me out.

The image of Riley in my room that afternoon jumped into my head. I remembered the way he had leaned into me, his dark hair falling into his eyes. How the corner of his lip had lifted in a smirk, and how he'd asked me if I really wanted him to leave.

A pleasurable shiver ran through me.

I didn't care if the guys weren't checking me out. There was only one person I wanted to be noticed by.

I pushed all thoughts of Riley to the back of my mind. It wasn't as though he was going to be here. A strange part of me was disappointed, as if the evening was a waste unless I saw him. I had to remember how shaken I was the last time I'd been in his company. How he'd threatened me...

Or warned me.

Either way, I couldn't help feeling like I should be worried. I should want to stay well away from both him and anyone else to do with the carnival. But then why was my soul drawn to him?

We entered the hall. Banners were strung across the walls and balloons had been tied in clusters to every pillar and post. On stage, a small band rocked out. A few people danced, but most stood around in groups. A bigger crowd had gathered around the front of the stage, and they jumped up and down in time to the music. A bar was set up on the opposite side of the room, serving non-alcoholic drinks. Of course.

We got our drinks and hung out on the outskirts of the dancers. Though it felt safer being the middle of the group, I had the feeling everyone else was doing the same as me, our gazes constantly drifting over the shoulders of our companions to see who else was here. A group of guys spotted us and headed over.

"Hey, Brooke," the leader of the gang said. He wore a big, loose sleeved shirt. Subtly, he lifted his arm and flashed what was hidden up his sleeve. A silver flask. "You guys want some of this?"

Brooke's face brightened. "Sure!"

Sneakily, he poured a shot of clear liquid, vodka, I assumed, into each of our drinks. The addition would do little to me. Alcohol didn't affect me. I hoped I wouldn't be holding the hair back from the faces of any of my new friends later that evening.

I spotted a familiar face. She wore a bow in her hair, bright red lipstick that looked classy on her, and a cute dress with a flared skirt.

"I'm just going to talk to someone." I excused myself from the others.

"Hey, Laurel," I said, shouting in her ear to get her attention over the band.

She turned with a smile which faltered when she realized who was speaking to her. "Oh, hey, Beth."

"Look, I wanted to apologize for not telling you the truth about what happened at the carnival earlier."

She shrugged. "Forget it. It's none of my business."

"I don't want you to think I'm some kind of pathological liar."

This at least elicited a small smile. "Not a pathological liar, but someone who can predict the future?"

She said it with no trace of irony in her voice, and something tightened inside me. What did she know?

A scream cut through the bass and guitars of the band. The singer fell silent first, followed by the guitarist and the final crash and bang of the drummer. Voices rose in concern, and students started moving around us, toward the place the scream had originated from. Laurel and I glanced at one another and followed the crowd to find out what was going on.

The students created a circle around a girl lying on the floor. Her body twisted and jerked, her eyes rolled in her head.

"Jesus!" I breathed. "Is she okay?"

Then, before I could think anything else, a number of the older students, Dana and Flynn included, swept in.

"Shouldn't someone call an ambulance?" I said, looking to Laurel, but she stood, transfixed on the scene in front of us. Her hand formed a fist at her mouth, her eyes wide and worried. She appeared more concerned than anyone else in the room, yet she didn't make any move toward the fitting girl.

Dana crouched beside the girl, waiting until the fit had finished, and then Flynn swept her up in his arms. As he lifted her, I noticed something fall from her fingers. The slip of metal dropped to the floor, and as the group moved forward, someone kicked it, sending it sliding in my direction. I don't know what made me do it, but I darted forward and picked the item off the floor, slipping it into the pocket of my jeans. Together, the older students walked from the hall, carrying the girl with them.

I realized the other girls, Brooke, Erin, and Kayla, were standing back around me again. We glanced uneasily at each other.

"Did she have a fit?" said Kayla. "Epilepsy, perhaps."

Brooke shrugged. "Or maybe she took something she shouldn't have? Perhaps her drink was spiked?"

The girls eyed their own cups nervously.

I noticed Laurel was particularly quiet, her line of sight still trained on the door where Dana and Flynn had carried the girl from the room.

Digging the item I'd picked up from my pocket, I glanced down. It was a silver necklace with some kind of pendant on the chain. I would have to try to find the girl and return it to her, though I was sure she had other things to worry about right now. I didn't want to go chasing after the group, waving the necklace around. I had attracted enough attention to myself already, and I didn't intend on creating any more. It was better if I slipped the jewelry back to her unnoticed.

I twisted the pendant in my fingers and frowned. The pendant was a silver circle with a star in the middle. I had seen a symbol similar to that before. The last time I'd come across it, magic had been involved.

Cold clutched at my heart.

"What have you got there?"

I turned at the sound of Laurel's voice, quickly closing my fingers around the pendant.

"Oh, it's nothing."

She laughed. "Don't be silly. I saw you pick something off the floor."

For some reason, an instinct perhaps, or maybe something else, I didn't want to show her. The pendant tingled and burned in my palm. I wasn't imagining that there was more to this piece of jewelry than just a circle of metal.

"A button pinged off my jeans," I told her. I gave a half-embarrassed shrug. "Guess I'd better start cutting down on that junk food."

She frowned at me, her eyes narrowing behind her glasses, and my cheeks heated, knowing she didn't believe me. My quip about me being a pathological liar was starting to feel like the truth.

Music started back up, and people began to close in around the gap where the girl had collapsed. Some couples started dancing again, while other stood in groups, chatting. But the mood of the party had grown subdued, as if an unseen force was pressing down on everyone. People smiled a little less willingly, danced with more reserve.

I kept my eyes peeled, trying to spot if Flynn or Dana returned to the party. I didn't see them inside the hall, so figured I'd try outside. I told the others where I was going, but Brooke barely glanced in my direction, and the other girls just nodded and smiled, and then continued their conversation. Probably sick of my lies, Laurel had taken herself off to talk to a different group of girls.

Deflated, I headed outside. The air was warm, but felt cooler than the muggy interior of a couple of hundred sweaty, hot teenagers.

I caught sight of the now familiar shape of Flynn's broad shoulders and buzzed head. He was sitting on the grass on his own, his back to me, looking out over the lit parking lot. I glanced to either side, but didn't see Dana anywhere. He appeared to be alone.

Breaking into a gentle jog, I headed over to him. His arms were rested on his bent knees, his feet planted on the ground. He must have heard me approach because he looked up at me with a frown.

"Beth. What are you doing out here? Shouldn't you be with your friends?"

I shrugged. "I don't think I know them well enough to call them friends yet." I experienced a pang of guilt for brushing off Laurel so easily. She seemed like the kind of girl I could be friends with, as long as I never inadvertently touched her.

I sat down on the grass beside him. "I just wanted to check that girl was okay."

"Melissa?"

"If that's her name."

"Yeah, she's fine. Dana is a first-aider, and she's taken her back to her room. She was coming around as soon as we got her out of the hall. It might have been the heat or something."

"Really? It seemed a lot worse than the heat. Shouldn't someone have called an ambulance?"

"Nah, no need to get the authorities involved. She was fine, I promise."

The necklace in my pocket seemed to vibrate. I wondered how long it would be before the girl—Melissa—would notice the chain was missing. I had a feeling she would panic when she did.

I needed to find out more before I gave it back to her. From experience, I knew that those connected with magic weren't always on the good side.

Something I'd considered earlier came back to me. I jerked my head toward the tall, expansive buildings of the dorms.

"So what's with all the names?" I asked, referring to the names each building had been given. "It's all a bit … herby."

He laughed, making his Adam's apple bob, and I relaxed slightly. "Goes back to when the town was first started. There's a rumor some of the founders of the town were into their herbal medicine, if you know what I mean?"

I pretended I didn't. "What, like drugs?"

"No, like spells and stuff."

"Witchcraft?"

"Oh, don't worry. It's only a few rumors."

Yeah, right. I knew where rumors came from, and pretty much all of them had at least one foot in reality.

He rubbed at his square jaw with one strong-fingered hand. He was just a little too perfect, I decided. Too much like a young, aspiring catalog model. Definitely not my type, if I even had a type. But there seemed to be something behind the good looks and the swimmer's body. There was a sharp glint of intelligence behind his green eyes.

"Seriously, Beth," he said, looking at me. "Don't worry about stuff like that. Just concentrate on getting good grades and doing what you want when you get into the real world."

I smiled. "You're parenting me again."

"I was, huh? I really must stop doing that if I ever want you to think of me as anything but a father figure."

I wasn't sure how to respond to his comment, but the roar of a motorbike, its headlight blazing, rolled into the parking lot. The rider stopped the bike suddenly, letting it fall to the ground as he climbed off. My eyes widened, and I jumped to my feet. Riley stormed toward us from the direction of the parking lot, his leather jacket flapping in the wind his motion created. His dark blue eyes appeared almost black in the moonlight, his expression grim.

My heart leapt in my chest, and I bit my lower lip in anticipation of what was to come.

Flynn got to his feet beside me. He radiated tension, his shoulders back, fists at his sides.

"Hey, Icy," Riley said, coming to a stop in front of us. He didn't smile, his eyes narrowed. The flirty demeanor he'd displayed in my room had vanished. He was deadly serious. "We've just had the cops come see us."

I stared back. "So what?"

"They've implied that you suspect the ride was sabotaged on purpose."

My mouth fell open. "What? I never said that!"

I tried to remember exactly what I had said. I'd been so desperate to get out of the cop car and away from them, I might have mentioned something about sabotage, though I was sure I'd quipped that I was the one who'd sabotaged the ride and then changed my mind. In hindsight, that probably wasn't the smartest of things I could have said.

"Yeah, well, now the guys I work for are seriously pissed. There's going to be repercussions, Icy!"

The tightness of his jaw made his cheekbones appear even sharper, his cheeks shadowed hollows beneath them. His blue eyes were big, fringed with dark lashes, though at that moment his appearance was more dangerous than anything else.

Flynn stepped forward. "Don't you threaten her!" he snapped, one finger pointed in Riley's face. "Your type shouldn't even be on campus."

Riley Draiodh was half a foot shorter than Flynn, and probably weighed twenty pounds less, but he didn't seem in the slightest bit intimidated.

His nostrils flared. "Yeah? And what exactly is my type?"

"A carny. Most of you are freaking criminals anyway!"

"Flynn!" I couldn't help my exclamation. His view shocked me.

Riley's head cocked to one side, and his eyes remained locked with Flynn's. "And what about what you are, huh?"

Alarm jarred through me, thinking Riley had somehow figured out about my half-vampire genetics, but then I realized he was still speaking to Flynn. What was he talking about?

Flynn shot him a warning glare. "Takes one to know one."

"What the hell are you two talking about?" I demanded.

"It's nothing," Flynn said, taking me by the upper arm to try to pull me away. I wasn't going anywhere.

"Anyway, I'm not here to fight," Riley said to Flynn. He turned to me. "I'm not threatening you, Icy. I'm trying to protect you. I tried to tell you before. The guys I work for won't put up with any shit. If they think you're going to be a problem for them, they'll make sure you won't get to open your mouth again. If the cops come to see you again, just tell them you don't know anything."

I threw my hands up in exasperation. "I don't know anything!"

Flynn stepped forward. "You heard her. Now get the hell out of here."

His interference was starting to get to me. While I didn't like what Riley was saying, I also didn't like Flynn hovering over me like some kind of over protective father figure. I already had one of those, and I'd moved thousands of miles away to create a life of my own.

"This doesn't have anything to do with you, Flynn," I told him.

"Someone needs to watch out for you."

I scowled, my annoyance ratcheting up a notch. "Don't give me that bullshit, and stop acting like either of you can protect me. If anyone is going to be doing the protecting around here, it's me. I'm stronger than the pair of you put together."

"Don't be crazy, Beth. You must barely weigh one hundred pounds."

I resisted the urge to growl at them. Instead, I clamped my teeth together to prevent myself spitting out the words, 'I'm half-vampire' just to see the expression on their faces.

I took a deep breath and tried again. "I'm trying to say that I don't need one baby-sitter, never mind two."

As if to prove my point, I stepped forward, pushing between them.

"Beth!" Flynn protested, but Riley said nothing. Even so, I sensed his gaze burning into my back as I walked away.

Don't look back, don't look back, I told myself, knowing so much as a glance would make me lose my cool.

CHAPTER 11

WITH MY HEART pounding, I stalked across campus, planning to go back to my room. The last thing I wanted was to get into a conversation with anyone else, but Erin and Kayla stood in the middle of the path ahead of me. I ducked my head down, hoping to somehow go unnoticed, but they'd already spotted me.

"Hey, Beth, there you are," Kayla said. "We wondered where you'd gotten to."

Erin frowned. "Everything okay?"

I forced a smile. "Oh, fine, thanks. I just got chatting with a couple of people, that's all." I noticed the threesome was missing one. "Brooke not with you?"

"Nah," Erin said. "She said she was tired, and went back to your room."

My heart sank. The last thing I wanted to do was go and hang out with Brooke. Hopefully, she had gone to bed already. I waved goodbye to the other girls and headed back to my room.

I stopped outside the door and placed my hand on the solid wood, intending to push it open. An image flashed through my head, making me gasp. *A couple of burly guys, both wearing wife-beater shirts and cheap tattoos, entered the room.* Was this a premonition or something that had already happened? As I opened the door and stepped through, another vision hit me. *One of the men lifted Brooke around her waist, her back pressed against his chest. She kicked out at the other man, but they both laughed.*

Oh, no.

Brooke wasn't in the room. The bedcovers were tangled and half spilled on the floor. An unusual scent filled the air, a combination of stale tobacco, sweat, and alcohol. The men had been in here. What I'd seen wasn't going to happen in the future. It must have only just occurred.

Shit.

I hesitated. What now? The men must have come from the carnival, here to warn me off personally. But why had they taken Brooke?

The worst fears ran through my head—strange men and a pretty, young college girl was never a good combination, at least not for the college girl. I remembered the card the cops had given me earlier that day. I'd flung it onto my nightstand when I'd changed earlier. It had quickly become lost among my books and other paperwork, but I rummaged through and found it. Fingering the soft cardboard, I thought hard. Should I call the police?

But what would I tell them? I hadn't seen anything, and Brooke was old enough to be out by herself. So what if her usually immaculate bed was a mess? Slovenliness was hardly a crime. I certainly couldn't tell them I'd had a vision of men coming into the room, and that I could still smell them on the air.

My other option was to go and find Flynn, and tell him I was worried about Brooke. After all, he'd been there when Riley told me about the carny guys being angry with me, though that still didn't explain why they'd taken Brooke and not waited for me. Had Brooke threatened to scream, or even *had* screamed, and so they'd needed to shut her up?

I trembled. Though I didn't have much love for the other girl, I never wanted to see her hurt, especially not because of me. Yet I remembered how Flynn had been toward Riley, a definite disdain for the carny folk. I didn't want him going in there, all guns blazing. I'd never find out anything that way.

I groaned and sank down to the edge of my bed, my forehead in my hands. I'd basically just convinced myself it was a good idea to head to the carnival and try to find Brooke myself.

No, I'll find Riley.

He might act like an asshole most of the time, but I was sure he'd genuinely been trying to warn as opposed to threaten me. The stupid, traitorous part of me couldn't help but be a bit excited at the idea of seeing him again. I wanted to be in his presence, that hint of danger, or darkness about him. I recognized it because it was in me too, drawing me toward him. I couldn't explain how everything dark, wicked, and gothic made my heart rate step up a notch, but in a good way. It was so unlike when I was in the presence of anything sweet or girlie. The darkness made me feel alive, true to myself. Real.

I pushed my thoughts away and forced myself to my feet. I took a breath, steadying my nerves. I'd do my best not to be noticed, but if I was, I needed to remember that I was stronger and faster than any of them. They might only see a slim, dark-haired, dark-eyed slip of a girl, but I could be wicked when I wanted to be.

Hoping not to be stopped by anyone, I grabbed my jacket and slunk from the room. I kept to the walls of the hallway, sneaking down into the stairwell to run the steps two at a time. I exited into the cool air, trying to spot any signs, physical or psychic, that might give me an idea about which direction Brooke had been taken.

I glanced around. Surely they couldn't have brought Brooke this way? Groups of students still hung out, chatting and laughing. A few gave me a fleeting look as I walked out, perhaps spotting my pallid face in the moonlight. If they'd brought her here, they'd have been noticed, and the alarm would have been called. But what other options did they have? Had our bedroom window been open again? I hadn't thought to check. The fire escape led down the back of the building, but I was sure the alarm would have gone off if someone had opened it, unless they disabled the alarm first.

With my head down, I walked at a fast pace toward the rental car I'd been loaned. I wished I had my old car back, wanting the comfort of slipping into the soft leather and 'new car' smell that reminded me of home.

The SUV would make me fit in better, especially around the carny guys, but that didn't stop me longing for home.

I could always call Mom and Dad.

But no, I didn't want to do that. My parents had taken care of me all these years. They'd spent time apart so I was never without someone in the daytime. I knew how hard it must have been for them. My mom, Serenity, had always been awake in the day to be with me, and then she'd needed to sleep when the night came and my dad, Sebastian, finally woke up. I was an adult now, and this was their time. They'd done everything for me, and I loved them dearly for it. I needed to repay the favor.

Climbing inside the truck, I turned the key in the ignition and started it up. The engine grumbled to life around me. I suppressed a smile, imagining what the rest of the L.A. crowd would have said if they'd been given this car as a replacement to their flash vehicles.

Yanking the shift stick into reverse, I slung my arm over the passenger seat and backed out of the lot. No one paid me any attention.

I drove down the road, the forest looming on one side, the buildings that made up Sage Springs on the other. Some buildings were still lit, but many now resided in darkness. My eyes were drawn back to the forest. Something about the tall pines seemed menacing, the spiky leaves reaching across the road.

Bypassing town, I took the route down toward the beach, planning on pulling over before I reached the parking lot where most of the carnival had been erected and walking the rest. It wasn't far. Within five minutes, I pulled the SUV over and parked beneath a tree, trying to ignore the rustling branches that felt like they were whispering a warning.

Moving quickly and almost silently on my sneakered feet, I hurried down the road, toward the carnival. No cars passed by, and I was thankful not to meet anyone else on foot either. I preferred to go unseen.

I rounded the bend, and the carnival stretched out before me. The line of the beach and the sea lay beyond, moonlight glinting off the waves. The shapes of the rides rose up into the moonlit sky like sleeping dinosaurs. It felt strange to see the place in darkness, void of bright lights, music and laughter. There was something creepy about the place now, threatening, though I suspected the vibrations I picked up were mainly caused by my knowledge that the people within might be dangerous.

The trailers where the carnies slept were positioned beyond the fairway. Lights beamed from the mobile homes, so I knew people were still up. Could one of the trailers contain Brooke? And which one did Riley live in?

Did he live alone, or with his parents? Hell, he might even live with a girlfriend for all I knew, though from the way he looked and spoke to me, I'd feel damn sorry for her if he did.

I snuck toward the entrance. Though a large gate blocked the way, it was all for show. No fencing circled the rides, or the area where the carnies lived. I could easily skirt around the gates and head onto the midway. Which is exactly what I did.

Running at a slow jog, I kept close to the big rides on my left. I allowed my fingertips to trail the cool metal of the sides of the rides and stalls, the Tilt-a-Whirl, a miniature rollercoaster, the Chair-o-Planes, as I passed by. On the other side of the midway, numerous stands to test people's skills, strength, and luck were partially covered with brightly colored awnings. Prizes of over-sized, over-stuffed teddy bears hung from almost macabre hooks. Adjacent to all the games and rides were the refreshments stands that should have been selling cotton candy, ice cream, funnel cakes and French fries. But instead, the place was dark and deserted, at a time when it should have been bustlingly busy, the carnies relieving all us marks of our money. I bet they were spitting blood at the loss of revenue.

I hoped to pick up on some kind of premonition or insight into the events that had happened around the rides, perhaps absorbing the energy of Brooke as she'd been dragged or carried past, kicking and screaming. For the first time, I realized I wanted whatever psychic screw-up my genetics had thrown at me to work. Normally, I dreaded picking anything up—it only ever seemed to get me into trouble—but if I could have made a giant glowing arrow appear above the trailer where either Riley or Brooke might be, then I would have.

Voices came, muffled and male, from somewhere in front of me. I ducked to my left to hide in the closest ride. Carousel horses were frozen at their points of gallop, legs lifted, and heads thrown back in a parody of a horse's freedom.

I crouched between two of the horses, my breath held. Two men walked past, one I recognized as the guy who had tried to help me from the car after the electric wire had fallen down. The other man I didn't recognize, but yet a shot of adrenaline fired through me at the sight of him. Something about the guy glowed a warning red to my psychic senses, and I was sure it wasn't just because of the way he looked. He was massive, his head, neck, and shoulders blending into one. Though where the man walking beside him was fat, this guy was all muscle. He moved with a swagger, his arms held to either side of him, his fists bunched, as though expecting a fight at any moment.

I strained to pick up on what the men were talking about…

"One of the busiest nights of the year, and we're sitting around with our asses in our hands."

"What else were we supposed to do? It's not like we could open up with the cops breathing down our necks."

"I know, but I still think shutting us down is overkill. Why not just shut the one ride…"

Their voices faded as they moved past me and continued down the midway. When they were far enough away, I allowed myself to exhale. They'd not shown any sign of knowing I was there, so as soon as they were gone, I slipped out from behind the horses, with their wide, wild eyes, and hurried on down the midway.

My ears picked up on a sound. It started as a hum, and developed into a low roar the closer I got. I don't know why I was drawn, but I moved toward the drone without even giving my actions a conscious thought.

The direction steered me away from both the midway and the trailers farther back where most of the carnies lived. I slipped between the sideshows—advertising kootch shows, fire eaters, and knife swallowers—and followed the sound. Set to one side was the source of the now loud roar. A huge metal mesh sphere was suspended several feet from the earth, metal poles and cables rooted into the ground. Inside the sphere, a motorbike roared around, looping vertically as well as horizontally. The bike whipped around so fast, the rider was almost a blur.

Mesmerized, I completely forget I was supposed to be hiding. The roar and whine of the bike as it zoomed around made me catch my breath and bite my knuckles. How was it even possible to ride upside down without the rider falling off?

As if my thoughts had somehow jeopardized him, the bike stuttered on its descent, and then skidded, the wheels spinning to one side. The rider just managed to catch himself before he was completely thrown. But still, he was dragged along the bottom of the sphere, one side of his body and head scraping against the metal. A scream almost burst from my throat, but I managed to clamp my mouth down around it, silencing myself. I couldn't help but run forward, unable to turn and leave someone who might be badly hurt, even if he was a carny and part of the people who had been threatening me and possibly abducted my roommate.

As I reached the sphere, the rider groaned and began to move. I banged on the wall with the palm of my hand. "Hey," I hissed, still mindful of where I was. "Are you okay?" I tried to see a door to the sphere, and ran around, my palms slapping against the metal until I located it. But the door was flush with the rest of the sphere, and I couldn't see a way to get it open.

The person pushed the bike off their body and started to sit up.

My heart almost stopped. I would recognize that dark hair and leather jacket anywhere.

"Riley?"

He got to his feet and ran a hand through his scruffy, jaw length hair. He looked at me with his head tilted to one side, squinting. A graze ran down one side of his face, the sight of the blood making my pulse pick up a rate, my mouth running dry.

"Jeez, Icy," he said bending to right his bike. His tone was cold, and I wondered if I should be the one calling him icy. "What the hell are you doing here?"

He unlocked a catch on the inside of the sphere and dragged his bike out.

I stared at him, still unable to believe what I'd seen him doing, but I didn't answer his question. Instead, I asked him one of my own. "Are you okay?"

"Of course I'm okay. I know what I'm doing. This is my job here."

"I thought you worked the Waltzer?"

He huffed air out through his mouth, puffing away a lock of hair that had fallen in his face. "That night, I did. I was covering for someone who'd gotten sick." His eyes narrowed. "You shouldn't be here. You need to leave right now."

Riley threw his bike to the ground. He turned and grabbed my wrist, meaning to pull me somewhere—away from the carnival, I assumed—but I planted my feet and refused to move.

His eyes widened in surprise at my strength, but he didn't say anything. Once again, I noticed I hadn't picked up anything psychically about him.

"I'm not going anywhere," I said. "Not yet. I need to ask you some questions."

"No. You need to leave. I'm not kidding."

"So, it's okay for you to come onto my turf, but I'm not allowed onto yours? Talk about double standards."

He glared at me, but something about my expression must have convinced him I was serious. "Okay, fine. But we can't stand out in the open like this. Someone could come along at any moment. My trailer's on the outskirts. As long as we keep quiet, no one should notice us."

"You live alone? I asked, fishing for information.

He gave me that narrow-eyed look again, the one that told me he was trying to figure me out. "Yeah, why?"

I shrugged. "Don't want anyone else to know I'm here, do we?"

He dropped his hold on my arm, but my skin buzzed where he had touched me. For once, this had nothing to do with my vampire side, and everything to do with being a teenage girl.

"Okay, come on then. Follow me. But if I lift my hand, it means stop. Okay?"

"Sure."

He set off at a fast walk, almost a jog, doing as I had only minutes earlier and staying close to the rides and stalls to avoid being seen. We were at the back of the stands now. The sound of voices and movement grew louder as we approached the large sprawl of trailers. Obviously wanting some modicum of privacy, the mobile homes were spread a fair distance apart, allowing for each of the carnies to live their home lives without worrying about being overheard by their neighbor. In fact, they had more privacy than I did in my dorm, or even most apartment-block living folks in town. A few people sat on foldout chairs outside their front doors, drinking or smoking, or sometimes both. They spoke in low voices, the mood somber, caused, I assumed by the fact they should have been working their concessions and earning much needed money, rather than hanging out. I tried to catch any sign of Brooke, or anyone who appeared on edge, or suspicious, but nothing caught my eye.

Riley had pulled up short right ahead of me. Distracted by the carny folk, I almost walked right into his back. I wondered what it would feel like to wrap my arms around his waist and press my cheek against his back, feel the soft leather of his jacket beneath my cheek, and inhale the scent of him. I shook my head at myself. Where the hell had that thought come from? I couldn't think of him that way.

He nodded toward a rundown mobile home right of the outskirts of the circle of homes. It would originally have been white, with a green trim, but was now a dirty shade of grey, the paint flaking off. Dirt caked the outside of the windows, and I shuddered to think what the inside would be like.

Riley leaned back to me and kept his voice low. "Move quickly and stay down. We don't want anyone to see us."

I glanced around to spot if anyone was paying us any attention, but everyone appeared to be too caught up in their own conversations to notice us. Even so, I did as Riley asked. We ran, with Riley just ahead of me, between the trailers and up to his place. A couple of metal steps led up to the front door, and he jumped up them, pulling the door open. I noticed he'd not needed to use a key to unlock the trailer. Whatever else he thought, he obviously trusted the other carnies.

I followed him inside, eagerly taking in the sight of Riley's home. The place was run down, second or even third hand cushions on the couch, which also served as a bench-type table. The material threadbare. A small kitchen was at the far end, the Formica tops scraped and scarred, many of the cupboards missing their handles. But the place was clean; no dirty dishes piled high in the sink, or overflowing trashcan as I had expected.

"Welcome to the palace," he said, his voice filled with sarcasm.

I offered him a smile, wanting to say something to make him more comfortable, for some reason, but struggling to come up with the words. After all, I grew up in a huge mansion in the Los Angeles hills. I wasn't naive enough to try to make out like Riley's place was anything more than what it was.

"Where are your parents?" I asked, curious.

Something in his face tightened. "Mom died when I was fifteen. Dad took off when I was four, I barely remember him."

"Sorry."

"Don't be. Wasn't your fault, was it?"

He turned away from me, busying himself in the kitchen. I had a feeling it was his way of changing the topic of conversation. He grabbed two tumblers from the cupboard and then pulled out a bottle of whisky. He poured two shots and handed one to me.

"I'd offer you some ice," he said. "But I don't have any."

I glanced down at the amber liquid and cocked an eyebrow. "Are you old enough to be drinking?"

"I'm twenty-two. I'm old enough to do whatever I want."

"You must realize I'm not old enough." I don't know why I said it—certainly not out of some moral code—more to see if it would get a reaction out of him.

He shrugged. "What the hell do I care?"

We stood a mere foot apart, but it could have been a gulf. There was a wall around him, a space I could feel but couldn't see. I don't know why I wanted to bridge the gap so badly, but I did.

I reached up and touched the graze that ran down beside his eye, toward his cheekbone. He didn't flinch away from me.

"You should clean that up," I told him.

My fingertips were smeared with red. I resisted the urge to put them in my mouth.

His eyes locked on mine, those deep pools of blue I could so easily lose myself in. "It's fine, Icy. Barely a scratch."

"My name's Elizabeth," I said, trying to remember to breathe.

I wanted to touch him again. I couldn't remember the last time I was with someone whose skin I didn't have to avoid. My palms itched, my fingers tingling. I knew I should wipe my bloodied fingertips on my jeans, but a dark part of me wanted the blood to dry there, so later, when I was alone, I could lift my fingers to my nose, and inhale the scent of his blood.

God, I was such a freak.

"So what are you doing here?" he asked, breaking the moment.

I glanced away, and took a drink of the whisky. The liquid burned down my throat, settling to warm my stomach. I fought not to cough. "My roommate has gone missing. I think some of your people had something to do with it."

He didn't bat an eyelash. "Probably."

I blinked in surprise. "Aren't you bothered?"

"Why would I be?"

"Err, because men can't just go around kidnapping college girls." I thought of something. "And anyway, you came to warn me that I might be in trouble. Why worry about me, but not about her?"

His eyes narrowed slightly, a crease appearing between his dark brows as though he were pondering something. "I'm not sure. You seem different."

That's because I am.

I wondered on what scale he'd picked up on there being something different about me. Did it have to do with my prediction of the accident, or was it something more, a kind of subconscious lean toward the paranormal part of me. The vampires I'd met, including my father, had all been charismatic, and some even beautiful—a perfect way for a predator to lure in its prey. I'd never considered myself to be either of those things, but for the first time, I wondered…

I folded my arms across my chest and frowned. "I need you to help me find her."

"Why would I do that, Icy?"

"Because I have no one else to turn to! The cops will laugh me off—"

His expression hardened. "You're not going to the cops!"

"The hell I'm not! If my roommate is missing and your guys are responsible, you can't actually expect me to just ignore it."

"He'll know if you do. Then he'll come for you, and it won't just be a warning."

I was starting to get angry now. Angry was never good. I lost control of myself when my emotions ran high, but I couldn't walk out now. "Who is 'he?' Tell me, dammit!"

"Bulldog Mackenzie. He runs the show. Folks round here call him 'The Bull.'"

Of course, the guy who'd walked past me, the one with the non-existent neck and the tattoos on his knuckles. He'd strutted down the midway like he'd owned the place. He'd not been in my vision about Brooke being taken, but I assumed he was behind sending the goons who did.

"He's got my roommate?"

Riley gave that nonchalant shrug again, and the red haze began to descend over my vision. My pulse thumped in my ears. I became hyper aware of the blood now drying on my fingers, and the blood growing dark and crusted on Riley's temple. I needed to get a hold of myself or I was going to do something I would regret.

Abruptly, I turned and shot toward the door. It slammed open under my palm and I almost fell down the steps.

"Icy, hey, wait up!"

Riley clearly hadn't expected me to turn and bolt in the middle of my questioning.

I ran back the way I'd come, skirting between a few of the mobile homes, before getting onto the midway and using the rides as shelter. I prayed Riley wouldn't start shouting after me, so getting me noticed. I also didn't want to bump into the guy I now knew to be the leader of the carnival, and the one behind Brooke's disappearance. I was also sure he had something to do with the accident which I had intervened on. He'd wanted something bad to happen, but why sabotage his own ride? He must have known it would get the place shut down and under investigation.

I didn't know, but I did know that I needed to get away from here. I might not be able to read anything about Riley, but something about him got my vampire side all hot and bothered. I needed to let my bloodlust cool down before I investigated any further. I wouldn't do anyone any good if I attacked someone, and it ended up being me who was under investigation.

Chapter 12

I WAS STANDING on the road on the outskirts of Sage Springs again, the town stretched out before me, the forest at my back. Something was different about the town, though at first I couldn't figure it out. The whole place was lit, bright lights glowing high into the night sky. But as I watched, the lights began to extinguish, at the furthest edge at first, but then creeping nearer and nearer, plummeting the town into darkness. A strange energy came from Sage Springs, an anti-energy, and I thought that if I got too close, it would somehow destroy me.

My heart beating hard, I turned my back to run away, planning on taking the road out of town, but the road was gone. In its place, numerous pine trees blocked my way, as if the forest had somehow closed in around me and swallowed the road.

I gasped and spun back around. I saw something I hadn't noticed before. One place was still illuminated in

Sage Springs. The carnival. The Ferris wheel was brightly lit, the huge wheel turning slowly, though no patrons sat in the buckets to enjoy the ride. The horses on the carousel lifted and dipped as they rode round and round and round, their backs bare, their nostrils flared and eyes rolling. I heard the clang of the bell as an invisible force hit the strong man game, and drove it home.

Lifeless. Everything felt lifeless. Empty. From the carnival that functioned as though filled, to the town left in darkness, to the empty people I'd seen before in my dreams. The only place that seemed to contain any depth, any soul, was the forest surrounding me, preventing me from leaving town.

I WOKE IN my dorm bed in a cold sweat and with the absolute, certain knowledge that something bad was going to happen in Sage Springs.

Sunlight poured in through the window, telling me it was time to get up. I could barely bring myself to think about class, what with Brooke missing and something bad going down at the carnival.

Movement came from the other side of the room, and I bolted upright, clutching my bedclothes to my chest. My first thought was that Riley had followed me and was in my room again, but as soon as I twisted around, I saw a familiar sheet of blonde hair and a curvy figure, pulling her long legs into a pair of jeans.

"Brooke?"

She turned her head to look over her shoulder at me. "Yeah?"

My eyes almost fell out of my head. As well as finding her back here, something else had changed as well. All over

Brooke's skin—the parts I could see anyway—her body was covered in symbols, intricately drawn onto her skin.

I sat up straighter and yanked off my blanket, swinging my legs out of bed to place my feet on the floor. In one swift movement, I was up and across the room. Brooke wore a light pink cardigan with her t-shirt, and I grabbed her, pulling at her clothing to try to find out if the markings were all over her body or not.

Brooke yanked away from me. "What the hell are you doing? Are you nuts?"

"Go and look in the mirror," I said. "Then you'll see."

Her expression went from angry to scared as she hurried over to a small sink in the corner of our room and the mirror above it. She twisted her head from side to side, inspecting her face, the worry never leaving her expression. She lifted her face to her hand to gently tug at her skin, as if searching for wrinkles that were yet to materialize.

She turned back to me. "I don't know what you're talking about."

My heart sank. She couldn't see the symbols.

"Where have you been all night, Brooke?" I asked her. She hadn't yet mentioned the carnies or the ordeal she'd been through the previous night.

She frowned. "I've been asleep, in bed, right here."

"No, you haven't. You weren't here when I went to bed, and now you are."

"You're lying. Everything must have caught up on me, 'cause I came over really sleepy at the social so decided to take myself to bed. I didn't go anywhere else!"

"You were taken to the carnival, don't you remember?"

Her nose wrinkled in disgust. "Are you on drugs, or something?"

She didn't remember. She didn't remember who had put the markings on her skin—markings it seemed she, and probably everyone else, couldn't see. I knew the carny people had something to do with this, but I didn't know what.

My roommate shook her head, and then turned her back on me and continued to get ready for class.

I remembered the necklace I still had. I pulled open my bedside drawer and checked to make sure it remained where I'd placed it for safe keeping. The little silver chain was there, nestled at the back. I pulled it out, meaning to inspect the symbol again, but the minute I did so, the invisible marks on Brooke's skin began to glow.

I stared at the spectacle.

"Would you stop looking at me like that," she snapped. "You're freaking me out."

I forced my eyes away. "Sorry."

Magic was involved here. I just had no idea as to what gain.

I held back from saying anything more to Brooke. She was bound to start telling others about all the strange things I did, and once again, attention would be drawn to me. Besides, I had class to get to.

Brooke didn't speak to me, or even make eye contact, though I couldn't help my own eyes being drawn back to all of the markings—circles with lines through them. A triangle with an extra line. Smaller circles joined together with more lines. A zigzag. An arrow. A circle with a dot in the middle.

I tried to compress them into my brain, planning to draw them as soon as Brooke left the room. I wanted more than anything to take out my smart phone and take a photograph of her, but I didn't think she'd exactly agree if I suddenly wanted to take some kind of best friend selfie.

Clearly wanting to get away from me, Brooke barely finished applying her makeup before she grabbed her stuff and left. The moment I was alone, I grabbed the notepad I always kept beside my bed for note-taking of dreams and other ideas, and started drawing. I spent too long trying to perfectly replicate the symbols I'd seen on her, knowing they would be important. I made myself late, barely having enough time to brush my teeth, throw on my clothes and yank my hair into a high ponytail.

I made it to my first class, barely. I sat through the lecture, trying to keep my mind on what was being said, while my thoughts kept drifting to Brooke, Riley, and the other carnies. Something was going on, but I couldn't figure out what. Was it possible Brooke had gone willingly with the carnies, and she'd lied about not knowing where she was? No, I'd seen her being dragged away in my vision. My foresight was a pain in the ass most of the time, but it wasn't often wrong. I felt like I should tell someone—the police, perhaps—but I knew I would only come out of the experience looking like a loon.

My dream bothered me as well. The emptiness of the town and the people residing in it. The menacing sense of the forest. The hint that the carnival was somehow caught up in it all. I couldn't tie it all together.

I'd brought the necklace with me, partly because I wanted to return it to its owner, but also because I figured it was connected to whatever the hell was going on. I wanted to find Melissa, the girl who'd had the fit at the party, and use the necklace as an excuse to ask her some questions. But also, I didn't want to leave the jewelry in my room in case Riley or the other carnies came and took it.

Unconsciously, I'd been fingering the necklace, twiddling the chain from finger to finger.

A hand snatched the piece of jewelry from mine, making me jump. "Hey!" I exclaimed.

I looked up to find Laurel in front of me.

"What the hell are you doing with this?" she hissed.

I blinked in surprise at the anger written across her face. "I found it on the floor the other night. I think it belongs to the girl who had the fit."

"I know it does." She glared at me. "You're not supposed to have it."

"Why? What's so important about it?"

For the first time, I considered whether Laurel knew something about what was going on around here.

"It's none of your business, but you shouldn't be taking other people's stuff."

"I didn't," I said, starting to get irate myself now. Laurel was acting as though I'd stolen it. "I found the necklace on the floor. I planned on giving it back as soon as I saw her again."

Laurel's fingers closed around the pendant, hiding the circle and star from my view. The fury that had been so apparent seeped away from her now she was in possession of the necklace. "No need. I'll give it back to her."

"How come you know Melissa?"

"I just do. She's from Sage Springs."

Hmm, something they all seemed to have in common. Everything strange I'd been faced with since coming here, had all originated with people from the town. No, that wasn't true. None of the carnies were from town. They were outsiders, just like me.

KEEPING MY HEAD down, my hands stuffed in my jean pockets, I headed toward the dining hall for lunch. My spirits were low, and I no longer cared if everyone was staring at me. Brooke, and probably her friends as well by now, hated me. Laurel had turned on me, probably because in her mind I was no more than a compulsive liar and possibly a thief. The whole town seemed to be hiding a giant secret, and I felt like I was the only person they were hiding it from.

I wondered again if coming here had been the right choice. I would never be like everyone else, no matter how hard I tried. At least with my parents, I'd been allowed to be myself.

Though I'd not eaten breakfast, food was the last thing on my mind, but I didn't know where else to go. Besides, my mom had bought me a meal plan, probably worried that I wouldn't eat if she didn't, and I felt bad not using the meals she'd paid for.

The thought of hunger made my mind turn to the events of last night, of standing with Riley in his home, touching the blood on his face. Heat blasted through me, coloring my cheeks and burning my insides. A sudden, desperate longing to be with him again filled me. Here I was surrounded by all the perfect people, the prom queens, and jocks, and cheerleaders, but I didn't want anything to do with them. With Riley, I sensed the darkness that so often coiled its way around me. I didn't feel like an outsider when I was with him. I felt like I was home.

Unexpected tears filled my eyes, and I blinked them away. How could I experience such a longing when I barely knew the guy?

A voice called to me, footsteps slapping on the ground from behind. I looked over my shoulder, wondering who had taken an interest in me. To my surprise, Dana was running toward me, her red hair flying. She came to a stop not far from me, her cheeks flushed, breathing a little harder than normal. I braced myself, expecting her to challenge me on something, but she smiled at me instead.

"Beth, I'm so glad I caught you! Flynn has a swim meet after class today. Any chance you could go along and write it up? I'm going to send our photographer as well."

I hadn't yet handed in my last assignment about Flynn. "What about the report on what happened at the carnival?" I thought she'd wanted me to write that up next.

"Oh, don't worry about that now," she said, waving her hand dismissively. "Old news."

The last thing I needed right now was the distraction of another report, especially since I hadn't even finished the last one. I wondered why she hadn't called me up on my tardiness, and why she wanted me around Flynn again.

"Are you sure I'm the right person to be doing the sports reports?" I said, trying to worm my way out of it. "To be honest, I don't know much about swimming."

"Oh, don't worry. Flynn can fill you in on any of the details you don't understand. Just add your own little sparkle to the words."

Sparkle? I wasn't sure I had any sparkle.

"Honestly, I'm sure someone else would be better doing it."

"No, Elizabeth," she said, her face hardening. "I want it to be you."

I didn't know why she was so insistent on having me as the reporter for Flynn's swim meet, but since Dana was the only person speaking to me as though I was a regular human being—even though I wasn't—I didn't want to tell her no and make her mad at me. "Sure," I relented.

"Great." She paused and then said, "Hey, Beth, you're okay, aren't you?"

"What do you mean?"

"I don't know, after the event at the carnival and everything. Being away from home for the first time. I know how things can get to someone when they're feeling alone."

I wondered what she'd heard about me that made her ask, but the fact she was being nice made me want to cry. "I'm fine, honest," I managed, though my voice sounded choked.

Dana gave me another smile. "Well, I'll speak to you later then." And she turned and walked off, her red curls bouncing as she went.

CHAPTER 13

THAT EVENING, I arrived at Sage Springs' Olympic-sized, outdoor pool. Already the stands were filling with people. I searched the crowds, chewing on my thumbnail, trying to spot either Flynn, or someone with a camera strapped around their neck who might be the Sage Gazette's photographer.

Someone handed me a program, and I glanced down at it, trying not to be baffled by all the names and numbers. *What the hell are seed times?*

"Elizabeth?"

A female voice came from behind me, and I turned to find the girl whose necklace I'd had until earlier that day standing there. My heart jumped, thinking she was going to start questioning me about what I'd been doing with her jewelry, but then I noticed the camera she held.

"I'm Melissa Wilder. I'm the photographer for the Sage Gazette. Dana said I'd see you here. I figured we should probably meet and make sure your story and my pictures worked together."

"Oh, sure," I stuttered. "It's nice to meet you."

"You too." She started to walk away, and I hesitated, unsure whether to follow, but she turned back and jerked her head in the direction she was going.

"There's a bench for reporters. We get prime seats. Perk of the job."

I smiled and followed, pretending this was something I already knew.

The place began to fill up, until almost every seat was taken. Another college had come in to compete against Sage Springs, and the two teams' supporters had naturally divided themselves between the two opposite parts of the stadium.

The swimmers began to file out of the changing room, some of them sitting on benches on the opposite side of the pool to where the reporters were, while others stood up, swinging their arms to warm up, or doing stretches.

My eyes automatically sought Flynn, but he was deep in conversation with another swimmer and paid no attention to me.

I focused on the program, trying to figure out which each of the columns of names and numbers meant. Wanting to appear busy, I took my notepad out of my bag and began jotting down my mental descriptions of the atmosphere and people.

Before I knew it, the swimmers were being announced. Guys lined up at the pool edge on the starter blocks.

"Take your marks… Get set…" and a whistle blew. In synchronized motion, the competitors dived into the water. Arms and legs thrashed, and they reached the end of the pool and flipped beneath the water, pushing back off the wall with their feet. All of the swimmers appeared to have reached the other side together to me, but the scores flashed up on the board, so someone must have been able to figure out who'd won.

For the next swim, Flynn's name was included in the announcement. He walked out into the pool area, swinging his arms and jumping up and down on the spot to warm up. He headed over to the pool and lined up with the other competitors, his toes curled around the edge of the starter block.

"Take your marks… Get set…" and the whistle blew once again. All the competitors dived in. The arena filled with the sound of people whistling and yelling their encouragement, but all of the noise faded into the background as I was mesmerized by Flynn's agility.

The water seemed to part before his fingers had even reached it, allowing him a clear path through. His powerful body cut through the water with barely a splash, keeping him an easy body's length ahead of all of his competitors. He literally appeared to be flying through the water, so streamline, his arms rising over his head to cut back through the water, his body undulating like a dolphin.

Excitement built in my stomach as he left the competition behind. I found myself jumping, clapping and screaming with everyone else.

Flynn won by a full body's length.

Facing me, he placed his hands on the side of the pool, and in one smooth move, pulled himself out of the pool to standing. He wore only a pair of very small, very tight swimming shorts, leaving nothing to the imagination.

"So, what did you think?" he asked me, catching his breath.

"You did great."

Don't look down, I willed myself. *Keep your eyes on his face.* "Better than great, in fact. You're really fast."

But I couldn't help myself, my gaze traveling down his lean torso. If Flynn Matthews dressed attracted everyone's attention, Flynn Matthews almost naked positively *demanded* everyone's attention.

He stood before me, water droplets coursing down his tanned skin, dripping from his golden hair and eyelashes. I couldn't help but stare. The curved muscles of his biceps and pectorals, the narrow line of his waist, broad shoulders and defined muscles. I gulped. I might not have much experience—boy-wise—but I was still an eighteen year old girl, well, part girl anyway.

"Thanks." He grinned and ran a hand over his head, shaking water from his hair.

Someone get him a towel, I wished vehemently. I looked around for one, hoping I could just cover him up myself. The effect he was having on me was simply not lady-like.

"So I assume you got the places our team made?" he said, completely unaware of my reaction to him standing almost naked in front of me.

I glanced down at my notes, happy to have something to distract me. "Oh, yeah, sure. But I could do with you explaining how the seeding arrangements work."

He nodded. "Sure. Let me get changed, and then maybe we can take a walk, or something. I like to cool down after a race."

Thank God, he was going to get changed. "No problem. I'll wait here, shall I?"

"Hang on, Flynn," called Melissa, lifting her camera high. "One more for the paper."

Flynn gave a boyish grin which managed to appear both sexy and shy, before he turned away from me to head off to the changing room.

I was staring again, but this time not at Flynn's fine body. Instead, something *on* his body had caught my attention. At the top of his back, midway between his shoulders and the base of his neck, was one of the symbols I had seen drawn on Brooke's body.

My mouth ran dry. I waited until he'd vanished from view and then rifled back through my notebook to where I'd drawn the symbols I could remember.

Yes, there it was. Exactly the same. It looked like a sideways flag, with a couple of smaller swirls coming from the base.

My heart sank. Was everyone in this town involved in something strange, or was it pure coincidence?

Melissa had sat down on one of the now deserted benches, flicking through the images on the screen of her digital camera. There wasn't any sign of the pale-faced girl, foaming at the mouth, her eyes rolling back in her head. This girl had it completely together. She'd made no move to touch me yet, not to shake my hand or anything else, but I wanted to touch her. Did she have the necklace on her now? Had Laurel told her that I'd taken it? If she had, Melissa wasn't giving any indication that she thought badly of me.

"Hey," I said, sitting down beside her. "Mind if I take a look at those?"

She gave me a half-frown, as if not expecting me to be quite so forward, but then said, "Yeah, sure," and handed me the camera.

I deliberately reached in too far as she passed it over, the back of my hand making contact with her fingers. I braced myself.

The necklace dropped into her hand. Her fingers curled around it, and she lifted it, pressing her fist to her heart. "Thank you," she said, her gaze lifting to take in Laurel standing in front of her. "Where did you find it?"

"That girl had it. The one we've been watching."

"What? How did she get it?"

"She picked it up off the floor when your chakras were thrown

out of line because of this damn planet alignment. You should be more careful."

"I was hardly in any state to be careful."

"I know, but something's off with her. She's involved with the carnival somehow. If we're not careful she could ruin everything..."

"Beth? Beth?"

I realized Melissa was speaking to me in the real world. I blinked, trying to regain focus. It wasn't often I picked up such clear visions. Normally they were only tiny glimpses. I could only assume it had something to do with the fact we'd all touched the necklace and had connected our energies somehow.

"Beth?" she said again. "Are you okay?"

"Yes, sorry. I'm a bit of a daydreamer." I pushed the camera back to her. "The pictures look great."

Flynn saved my awkwardness by choosing that minute to return. He stopped right in front of me. "Okay, ready?" he asked.

Melissa squinted up at him, and then back at me, clearly wondering what the deal was.

"I'm just getting some details for the article," I said, not sure why I felt the need to explain myself to her.

She lifted her eyebrows, a small smile on her lips, and gave a nod that said, 'sure you are.'

I got to my feet, stepping into Flynn's side. I sensed eyes watching as we walked from the pool and out onto campus. The image of the tattoo on his upper back played on my mind. Did it mean Flynn had something to do with whatever happened to Brooke?

"So where do you want to walk to?" I asked.

"How about a hike out through the forest? Not too far, but enough to get away from all the people. Having everyone shouting like that for the last hour makes me want to escape to somewhere quiet."

I wanted to suggest the library as being a perfectly decent, quiet place in which to talk, but didn't want to appear to be a total nerd. Besides, though my dreams had pointed toward the forest as containing something threatening, I couldn't avoid the place forever.

"Sounds great."

I wondered how sensible it was to go walking in the middle of a forest, in the evening, with a boy I thought might be connected with the kidnapping of my roommate, and the occult drawings I found on her body. Yet I considered myself to be a fairly good judge of character, and I didn't get any sense of darkness coming from Flynn. Not like Riley. I felt a stab of guilt at the thought of Riley, though the guilt was misplaced. After all, attraction alone didn't give you a hold on another person.

Anyway, I doubted Flynn could do me much harm, even if he wanted to. In reality, I was more likely to hurt him than the other way around. My control over my bloodlust seemed to be getting weaker by the day. I wondered if it was this place that was causing it, the people I was around, or perhaps it was just me.

We headed off campus and turned a couple of blocks until the road led to a forest trail. Flynn walked with long, strong strides, and I hurried to keep up. We headed out along a trail into the forest. It was peaceful this time of the evening, the heat of the sun waning, insects buzzing around our heads. I swiped at a couple of mosquitoes which whined by my ear, though I didn't want to kill the bugs I shared an evolutionary trait with.

Flynn slowed, allowing me to catch up. "So, have you seen that carny guy again?" His tone was terse, and I felt myself bristle. Was this the reason he'd brought me out here?

"No," I lied. "Have you?"

He glanced at me, confused. "Why would I have?"

"Why would I?" I snapped back.

He shrugged. "I don't know. I guess he seemed kind of interested in you."

"That doesn't mean I'm interested in him." My voice was sharp. I couldn't help myself.

He held up his hands in mock submission. "Okay, okay. No need to get defensive."

"Anyway," I said, "aren't we supposed to be talking about swimming?"

"Sure. I just wanted to show you something first."

Alarm spiked through me. Was this where it was all about to go wrong?

Flynn stepped off the track and moved between the huge trunks of the old pine trees, ferns brushing against his legs.

I hesitated.

He turned back to me. "You coming?"

I'm fast and strong, I reminded myself. *If he tries something, I'll rip his throat out.*

I widened my eyes, staring down at the ground, shocked at myself. Where the hell had *that* thought come from?

We seemed to be walking in a random direction through the forest, not sticking to one trail or another, but Flynn moved with certainty, as if he knew exactly where he was going. We cut between the tree trunks, birds settling in the branches overhead to roost for the night. The heat of the day had waned, and where the foliage grew dense, casting deep, thick shadows onto the forest floor, the air almost became chilly. In the distance, I became aware of a noise—a low thrumming and grinding of machinery, though it seemed to be coming from below us.

I frowned. "What is that?"

"The noise, you mean?"

I nodded.

"It's the Squires Mining Corporation. They own and mine most of the land around here. When they're not digging up the ground, they're chopping down the trees to make wood pellets for fuel."

"Oh, right," I said, my thoughts already drifting. Was this the same company Brooke said her parents owned? I hated to think of the beautiful forest being destroyed like that.

"How much farther?" I asked, trying not to get worried. We seemed to have been walking for awhile, and I felt like I'd completely lost any idea about how to get back.

"Almost there."

We stepped into a clearing, and my breath fell away. Several pools of water were dotted around the clearing, each one a similar size, except one, larger pool in the center. They were perfect ovals of still, glass-like water. They seemed almost manmade, the way the edges of the pools met the forest floor. A few rocks crested the sides, but otherwise they appeared to be perfect. The water was an aqua green, almost exactly the same shade as Flynn's eyes.

I turned to Flynn. "What is this place?"

His gaze cast over the pools, a proud smile on his face. "Just part of the forest I found."

But there was something more, I could sense it. The very air seemed to hum, the plants and flowers too perfect. I felt as though I'd walked into a painting, something that appeared to be real, lifelike, yet wasn't.

"I brought you here for a reason, Beth."

His voice broke me from my thoughts. I turned to look at him, half expecting him to be wielding a knife, or a length of rope. But the expression on his face wasn't murderous. "You did?"

He stepped in closer to me, closing the gap. "I like you. Haven't you figured that out yet?"

"What?" His words came out of the blue, making me step back, widening the space between us again. Of all the things I'd been expecting him to say, it wasn't that.

Flynn frowned. "Why do you seem so surprised? I've been hanging around, trying to get your attention, wanting to watch out for you. You're smart, and spiky in a kind of frustrating way at times. You're crazy beautiful, but you don't dress to show off like all the other girls."

I blinked. "What?"

"Would you stop saying what?" he hissed in frustration.

I could barely believe what I had heard him say. "I'm sorry, but you think I'm beautiful?"

He laughed. "Of course you are. With those amazing, big dark eyes and your pale skin, and all those dark curls. You look like a cross between Bambi and a porcelain doll."

I almost had to laugh at his description. "And you think that's beautiful?"

"More beautiful than any other girl I've ever seen."

His words snatched my breath from my lungs. How was Flynn Matthews—the guy at school every girl wanted to be with, and every guy wanted to be—standing here, saying this stuff to me? I remembered how he'd looked with his clothes off, water streaming down his tanned body. I'd be crazy to turn him down. But I had to. While I couldn't deny that I was physically attracted to Flynn, I had three problems. The first was that the barrage of images I suffered with every day wouldn't do anything to nurse a healthy relationship. The second was that I still didn't know what Flynn's involvement was with Brooke's missing night. And the third was that, though I liked Flynn, he didn't make my emotions surge in the way Riley did.

I shook my head. "I'm sorry, Flynn. I'm not sure I'm ready for all of this. I mean, I only just got to Sage Springs. A lot has happened…"

His aqua eyes darkened a shade. "It's that carny boy, isn't it?"

I detected anger in his voice.

"No!" I said, though I couldn't help but wonder if that was a lie. If Riley had never entered the picture, would I be falling into Flynn's arms? *Yes, but if you did,* a little voice said, *what would you see of him?* "Nothing has happened between Riley and me."

"But you want it to."

"I don't want anything right now! I just want to settle down to my studies and be a normal college student."

"That boy is dangerous, Beth."

"What do you know? You don't even know him!"

"I don't need to know him, I know the people he is with. You stay away from them, do you hear me?"

He reached out to grab my arm, and I jerked away. "You don't have any say in what I do."

"Get real, Beth! Why the hell won't you listen to me?" His anger was building, his square jaw strained.

From out of nowhere, my hair suddenly lifted and whipped around my face, my clothes blowing hard against my body. Above my head, the branches of the trees rustled and swayed. The wind had started as suddenly as if someone had placed a wind machine beside us.

Water splashing made me turn my head. Each of the pools were no longer still, waves rose and crashed on the edges, some splashing onto the forest floor.

"What the hell?"

Flynn followed my line of sight and paled beneath his tanned skin. "Come on, let's get out of here."

"Hang on a minute. What's going on? Those pools were still as glass a moment ago."

"Must be the wind," he said, grabbing my arm and pulling me back toward the trees.

"Where the hell did the wind come from?" I allowed myself to be pulled this time, freaked out by the waves lifting seemingly from nowhere, slapping and splashing. The gusts lifted leaves from the forest floor and blew them like tumbleweeds. The trees strained against the wind's strength.

As we moved through the trees, I glanced back. The blustery weather had fallen still as quickly as it had started. The pools were once again motionless mirrors. If it wasn't for the dark patches marking the ground around them, where the water had dampened the soil, I would have questioned if I imagined the whole thing.

Chapter 14

WE MADE OUR way back to campus in silence, neither mentioning the strange event at the pools, nor Flynn's declaration for me.

It had fallen dark by the time we returned to the dorms, though the night was clear, the stars bright in clusters above our heads.

Only after Flynn said goodnight and left me outside my dorm, did I realize I'd never had a chance to ask him about anything to do with swimming. I must be the worst reporter in the world, and Dana was surely never going to ask me to write her an article again. The second thing that dawned on me was that I hadn't seen anything about Flynn when he'd grabbed me to pull me away from the pools.

I didn't always get glimpses into people's pasts and futures every time they touched me, but the number of times I'd not gotten anything from someone over the past few days was unusual.

I'd made out to Flynn that I was heading back to my room, but my head was spinning way too much to go to bed. I'd never been more awake. Though we must have walked several miles through the forests, I felt jittery and alert—as though I'd downed a couple of cups of coffee too many. Once again, I found myself wanting to avoid my room because I didn't want to face Brooke. She was probably at a party or some other social, but I didn't want to risk happening upon her and discovering the symbols on her skin hadn't faded over the day. I wondered what they'd been drawn in—obviously not pen or chalk, as other people and Brooke herself would have been able to see them. Maybe some kind of sap my vision could pick up on? Or maybe I'd been able to pick up on some kind of psychic trace where someone had simply marked the shapes out on her skin with their finger. Perhaps they didn't exist at all. I'd simply seen a trace of where someone else's energy had touched her skin.

I waited until I was sure Flynn was well out of the way, and then headed down toward the car lot. Did I want to drive? No, not tonight, I needed to burn off some energy. I wondered when I would get my old car back. It had been a few days now and I'd not heard anything. The garage said it would be a while to get the parts in—seemed they didn't keep many parts for an Audi around here.

Pocketing my keys, I started to walk. This time I stayed on the main road, heading down toward the beach. I told myself I was avoiding the forest, but the truth was that every step took me closer to Riley and the darkened carnival.

Full headlights blazed in the road ahead, making me squint and lift my hand to cover my eyes. The car was going too fast, and I stepped away from the curb, sure this was a gang of guys out joyriding, probably with a few beers already consumed. The car screeched to a halt right beside me, and my heart catapulted into my throat. I didn't stop, but picked up my pace. I wanted to break into a run, but the sensible part of me prevented me doing so in case they'd simply stopped to ask for directions, and I made a fool of myself by running down the street in a panic.

Three big guys, all in their late twenties to mid-thirties, jumped from the car and headed straight for me. They moved with surprising speed, staring at me with anger and violence in their eyes. I realized they knew exactly who I was. They hadn't driven past me by accident, they'd come to find me. These guys were from the carnival. I thought I recognized one of them as the man who had been talking to Bulldog Mackenzie when I'd last been at the carnival. I opened my mouth to scream for help, but before I could get any sound out, the biggest of the men jumped me, punching the air from my lungs. I gasped, but barely had time to breathe again before he'd grabbed me around the neck and slammed me up against the wall which ran parallel to the sidewalk.

Pain rocketed through my back and ribs. I would have cried out, but I still had no air, and the man's thick, sweaty fingers wrapped around my throat, throttling me. A flash came to me; the man who had hold of me was crouched down before a couple of big slabs of metal. In his hand he held a screwdriver, and he lodged the point of it into one of the screws in the slab and began to twist. But he didn't unscrew it all the way. Instead, he only loosened it, though enough for the thread to be showing, and then moved onto the next. Something made a noise and he looked around, sharply. Now I could see the rest of the picture—painted clown's faces leering down, brightly colored swings, flashing lights—and everything fell into place. He was at the carnival, and he was loosening the screws in the Waltzer. A voice came from beside him, 'You done what we discussed, Jordy?' He nodded. 'All done, Boss.'

I blinked and the scene vanished, only to be replaced by the all too real one in front of me.

"You've been at the carnival again, poking around," he said, his face only inches from mine. His spittle hit my skin as he spoke, his rancid breath—like old meat—washing over my face. "People have seen you there."

"Let me go!" I managed to choke out, my voice strangled.

"Keep your mouth shut, little girl, or we're going to shut it for you. Permanently."

Where was everyone? I prayed for a car to drive by, or for some other college students to come walking down the road, perhaps heading to the beach for a party, or even to make out, or skinny dip. But the road was deserted apart from me and my three friends.

No one else was going to get me out of this situation. I needed to save myself.

Remember who you are. What you are …

Red descended over my vision. "Yeah," I managed to spit back, recovering my breath. "Just you try it!"

The guy glanced over his shoulder, his eyes widening, a sneer of a smile spreading over his fat, smug face. His buddies laughed, *haw haw haw*, as if this whole thing was nothing but a big joke.

He turned back to me. "This is going to be a pleasure."

I held back, wanting to strike at exactly the right moment. I might have my strengths, but there were still three of them and one of me, and each of them alone outweighed me three times over.

"She's old enough, right, Jordy?" one of the other guys called.

Jordy sneered again. "Just about. Not that it would matter too much, though."

"Drag her behind the wall," the other guy suggested. "No one will see us then."

Jordy was already pulling at his belt, unbuttoning his fly. "I get to go first. I ain't having your sloppy seconds."

Bile filled my throat. Did they really mean to do what I think they did?

Jordy released my throat. He pushed me to the side, shoving me down the sidewalk so he could get me behind the wall which divided the road from the adjoining scrubland. While I didn't want to be taken out of sight of the main road, if I was forced to do something extreme, I wanted to be seen by the general public even less than they did.

They surrounded me like dogs around a lamb.

My mouth ran dry, my throat closing over with a familiar, painful tightening. But my body's reaction had nothing to do with fear. Everything grew loud, my senses sharpening. Still I waited, a predator's instinct of dividing the weak from the strong in a herd. They thought they were dealing with the lamb, when actually they were dealing with the wolf.

"Go keep watch, Mitch," Jordy said. "You too, Russ. I don't need a goddamned audience."

I'd been fighting this for so long, doing everything I could to take myself out of situations that elicited the blood lust. I'd even resorted to hurting myself in order to stop the urges. But right now, the feeling of power, and hate, and want, and need built up inside me. And I let it. I focused solely on the purple veins crawling the way up this man's thick neck, pulsating slightly with the heart beat. The thump settled in my veins, my heart rate growing faster to align with his. I knew nothing else in the world except the feeling in my mouth, the thirst which hurt my throat, and the throbbing of this man's pulse.

I hadn't even noticed that he'd pushed me backward, while he finished unbuttoning his pants and unzipped his fly. The last thing I wanted to see was what he had in there.

My gaze slipped over to where the other two men had disappeared behind the wall, keeping an eye out for anyone who might help me, or report them.

"Come on, baby," said Jordy, his upper lip curled. "You want to know what a real man feels like?"

I stared at him, cold, hungry.

The expression on his face changed. He opened his mouth to yell for his friends, but I didn't give him the chance.

I shot forward, heading for the jugular. I had always thought I would experience some kind of shame or disgust, but in that moment I thought nothing. My mouth closed around the skin of his throat and my teeth—teeth that had once been small and blunt—clamped like a bear claw trap into his throat. Blood flowed, an iron river on which every sense I'd ever experienced was carried. Jordy gave a few strangled cries, but the sounds were no more than he might have made during orgasm—not that I had any experience on that front.

I sucked and swallowed, and swallowed, and swallowed again.

"Jordy?" one of the men called out. "You done yet? We're getting impatient over here!"

Obviously, they got no answer.

I lifted my face from his throat.

Jordy felt like a rag doll in my arms. With his blood flowing through my veins, I was stronger than I'd ever been. I barely even noticed I still held him up.

One of the guys, Russ, came around the corner.

His eyes widened in horror, and he staggered back. "Jesus Christ!"

Like a wild cat, I curled my bloodied lips at him, and snarled. He spun on his heels, almost falling, and reeled away from the scene in front of him.

I heard Mitch's confused tone. "What's going on?"

"Just get out of here!"

"What? What about Jordy?"

"Forget Jordy! Just go!"

Car doors opened and slammed, and the engine roared to life. The wheels screeched against the asphalt, and the sound of the vehicle faded into the distance.

I considered going after them, but my blood lust had been sated, and I wasn't sure what I'd do with them even if I caught them. I had a body to deal with, and absolutely no idea what to do with it.

Would they go back and tell everyone what I did?

I lifted my hand and wiped my mouth. Red streaked my pale skin. Abruptly, I turned to one side and vomited, the blood projecting from my mouth as though a faucet had been switched on. I coughed and spluttered, my eyes streaming. I barked a sob. What the hell was I supposed to do now? I was a killer.

Blood was everywhere, seeping down my chest and soaking into the ground. I hadn't made two neat, little puncture holes in the man's neck. Instead, a huge chunk of his flesh was missing, leaving a bloodied, raw, gaping wound from which his life force still continued to ebb.

I wasn't just a freak. I was a monster.

Memories came pouring back to me. I'd tasted blood as a child, too. I remembered.

Sinking to the ground, I cried until my throat hurt. I was waiting for the carny guys to come back and bring the cops with them. I would spend the rest of my life in jail.

I didn't know how much time passed, the body of my victim rapidly cooling beside me. The moon crossed the sky overhead, the occasional voices or footsteps passing by me on the other side of the wall, before fading away. Until eventually, the hour grew so late—or perhaps so early—that the rest of the world slept.

The grumble of an engine lured me out of my grief-stricken haze. The sound grew louder as it approached, and then slowed and stopped on the other side of the wall. I steeled myself. This was it. They were coming to get me. I wasn't even sure I wanted to fight any more.

I looked up to see who had come for me—Bulldog Mackenzie, or even the cops—but instead Riley stood before me in his leather jacket, his jaw-length hair hanging in his face, his dark blue eyes darting in horror between me and the bloodied mess of a body I had left.

"Jesus, Icy. What the hell happened?"

I stared back at him and then glanced at the body at my side. Jordy's face was white in the moonlight, drained of blood, his eyes still open and staring. The gaping hole in his throat appeared black.

"He … He attacked me," I managed, before the tears took hold again. Before I knew what was happening, Riley was at my side, crouched to my level. He gathered me up in his arms, pressing my face to his chest, so I inhaled the musty scent of his leather jacket.

"Shh," he said, the palm of his hand pressed against my hair. "It's all right. It's all going to be all right."

Why was he doing this, holding me? He should be running right now, and screaming like hell, letting everyone know about the monster in their midst.

"It's not okay," I sniffed. I wanted to move away from him,

but at the same time, I didn't ever want to let go. "I killed a man."

Riley leaned to one side to get a look at Jordy again. "And a damn thorough job you did of it too. How did you do that, Icy? It looks like you ripped his throat out."

That's 'cause I did…

I forced myself to move away from him, though my soul cried out at the feeling of space between us again. "I can't get you involved."

"Don't be crazy. I already am involved."

"You should be furious at me. Why haven't you called the police already?"

"It was self-defense, wasn't it? Anyway, carny people don't get the cops involved, ever. We handle our own business."

I sniffed again. "But I'm not a carny."

"No, I am. And you're my business now."

"Why?"

He scowled at me. "Stop giving me an argument every time I open my mouth. Now do you want help or not?"

"I want help," I admitted, my voice tiny.

"Good. I know somewhere we can go to get rid of the body. Just wait here one minute."

I didn't want to be left alone again with Jordy's corpse, but I forced myself to keep my mouth shut, not wanting to give Riley a quarrel, and so proving him right about my argumentative skills.

Within a minute, Riley was back, dragging his bike with him. "This is going to be awkward, and a bit gross, but I can't think of any other way. We'll haul him onto the front of the bike. I'll sit behind the body, and you sit behind me, okay? You'll have to hold on tight, 'cause you're not going to have any seat space, and we're going to be off-roading. Got it?"

"Got it."

I didn't want Riley to mess up his bike with Jordy's blood, though most of it was no longer in him. But I knew trying to convince him to do something else wouldn't work, so I said nothing.

"How strong are you feeling?" he asked.

"Strong." He had no idea how strong.

Together, we lifted Jordy and positioned his body over the handlebars, his torso slumping forward, arms hanging down, his fat ass positioned on the seat. Riley sat astride, having to effectively wrap his arms around Jordy's body in order to reach the handlebars.

He kicked the bike into life, and I climbed on behind him. My stomach roiled with nerves.

Riley headed away from the wall and the road, crossing the scrubland and a field to head deeper into the forest. We bumped and jolted across the rough terrain, the body occasionally slipping so we had to stop and readjust it. Riley handled the bike with impressive skill, leaning when needed, slowing down or speeding up at other times, like a horse rider who understood his animal on an instinctive level.

I had to force myself not to take pleasure in my close proximity to Riley, knowing there was a dead man right in front of us, and that his blood still coated my clothes. It was hard work trying to have the reactions and thought processes of a normal girl, when every part of me knew I wasn't.

CHAPTER 15

I BARELY KNEW the forests surrounding Sage Springs, but I trusted my sense of direction. Though Riley weaved the bike between the trees, often having to change his route due to a fallen log or a clump of bushes, I had a sickening sense that I knew exactly where he was going. Was I picking this off him psychically? It was possible, I was after all, physically closer to him than I'd ever been to another male—except perhaps my dad—right now. But I couldn't help feeling as though the place itself was sending me a psychic calling.

Closer, you're getting closer...

I clung tighter to Riley's jacket. I wanted to tell him to stop, to go back, but I couldn't. What would I say? That I had a strange feeling about the place I somehow knew he was taking me to?

Within half an hour, I was proven right.

Riley roared the bike into the clearing, and once again I was faced with those strange, glass-like pools. No insects buzzed around the water. Even in Riley's bike headlights, where they'd been swarming on the drive here, attracted by both the light and the blood from the body, now there were none.

As soon as we stopped, the bike tilted to one side and Jordy's body tumbled off, landing in a crumpled heap on the ground. Riley glanced back at me, and must have assumed my pale, worried expression was due to the presence of the corpse.

He placed his hand on my arm, rubbing me in comfort. "Don't worry. He'll be gone soon. He won't ever bother you again."

"Unless someone finds the body."

"They won't."

"What makes you so sure?"

"Because things go someplace else when they're here."

Goosebumps crawled up my skin. "What are you talking about?"

"I just know that when things go into these pools, they don't ever come back. Now give me a hand." He bent to the body and started to drag it toward the nearest pool.

The place was beautiful, still and majestic, and otherworldly. Yet I sensed something predatory about the place. Like the vampires I was so familiar with, the clearing of pools seemed to lure unsuspecting people in with its beauty, only to bite when least expected.

"Riley," I said, sudden panic heightening my voice. "Be careful."

He misunderstood me. "Don't worry. He's dead." I opened my mouth to try to explain, but I didn't know how to voice my concerns. They sounded crazy, even in my own head. Instead, I bent to grab Jordy's fat ankles, and, with Riley leading by lifting his arms, we dragged him closer to the nearest pool.

"Don't get too near it," I said. "You might fall in."

He laughed, but the sound was cold. "I think that's the least of our worries, Icy."

I wasn't so sure.

Riley dragged him the rest of the way, tipping Jordy's body off the edge. The corpse dropped head first off the bank, slipping into the water like a seal off a rock.

Wouldn't he float?

I voiced my thoughts to Riley, but he shook his head. "Not here. Nothing floats here. It's like the water sucks them down."

"I knew I didn't like this place," I muttered beneath my breath.

The rest of Jordy's body vanished beneath the water. I had to admit, I was pleased to see him gone.

Riley turned to me. "Now your clothes."

I gaped at him. "You've got to be kidding me?"

"You're covered in blood, Icy. You need to get rid of those clothes."

He was right. "Shit."

"Keep your panties on," he said, a smile tugging at his lips, a teasing note to his tone. "I mean that literally, of course. There won't be any blood on them."

I wore jeans, which were soaked through. The blood may have made it down to my underwear, but I prayed it hadn't. I huffed air out through my nose.

"Okay, fine. But you're lending me your jacket, okay?"

"Sure. You in your panties and my jacket sounds good to me."

I glared at him, but there was nothing else I could do. "Turn around, will you?" I snapped.

He gave me that knowing look again, and slowly turned his back to me. I glanced back at the pool nervously, half expecting the waves to start back up, or for Jordy's body to float slowly and silently to the top, his eyes glassy and staring. But the water remained still.

"Hey," I hissed at him, remembering something. "Your jacket."

He turned back to me, grinning, and shrugged off the leather coat. He took a couple of steps toward me, and handed it to me.

"Thanks," I said, though my gratitude was begrudging.

"Any time." He stood there, grinning at me.

I widened my eyes. "Turn around!"

He laughed, but did as I asked. Even so, I was horribly aware of his presence, perhaps even more so than the presence of the pool directly behind me. I quickly pulled my top over my head, and glanced down at my bra. Dammit. The white lace was pink with blood. I had no choice but to take it off. Before I did so, I kicked off my sneakers and yanked my jeans down my legs. The material had grown hard and crusted, and I struggled to get them off my thighs. Anxiously, I checked my panties for any sign of blood, twisting my head around and arching one leg to try to get a decent look at my ass. As far as I could see, the blood hadn't made it through the thick denim.

A breeze stirred around me, ruffling my hair.

"Throw the clothes in the water," Riley called out to me.

My heart almost stopped. Had he been watching me after all? But no, his back was still turned.

"Shit," I said again. I gathered up my clothes and dumped them into the pool, being careful to keep my toes away from the edge, still worried something would reach out and grab me, or else the water itself would suddenly rise in a wave and wash me in. The jeans and shirt quickly sank into the still depths. I hesitated and then reached around my back and unclipped my bra. The cool night kissed my skin, making my nipples pucker. With one arm covering my chest, I threw the bra into the water to join the rest of my clothes.

I snatched Riley's jacket up from where I'd let it drop. It was big on me, thank goodness, big enough to hang just past my butt, and cover some of my thighs. I zipped it up, covering my exposed breasts, thankful for my return to modesty, and comforted in the feeling of being covered by Riley.

I blushed at the thought. "Okay, I'm done."

He turned back to me and smiled, his gaze traveling up and down my body. "Looks good on you, Icy."

"Oh, shut the hell up."

I glanced down with sadness at my much loved sneakers. The soles were covered in blood, the canvas tops saturated. They wouldn't be coming back with me. I sighed and bent to pick them up, before slinging them into the water to join the rest of my clothes, and the man I had murdered.

"Come on," said Riley, jerking his head toward his bike. "Let's get out of here."

Barefooted, I ran back toward his bike. Riley swung his leg over the seat and kicked the bike into gear. I hopped on after him, able to scoot closer on the seat this time, and wrapped my arms around his waist to hold on. The position made the jacket ride up, so it sat at my hips, and did nothing to cover my thighs or panties. I couldn't worry about that now, though Riley glanced down to give my naked thigh an appreciative stare.

The bike jumped forward, and Riley turned the machine in a tight circle, before heading back the way we'd come. We were able to make faster progress this time, and we bumped and lurched across the uneven terrain, causing me to hold on tighter. I couldn't help myself. I pressed my face against his back, feeling the heat of his skin through the thin t-shirt he wore, the only item of clothing covering his torso now that I was in possession of his jacket. The roar of the bike through the otherwise silent forest sent nocturnal animals skittering for cover. The bugs were back again, flitting in the headlights of the motorcycle. I took comfort in their return. We had moved beyond whatever strange realm of power the pools held.

It was the early hours of the morning by the time we made it back to campus. I didn't want to have to go to my room, but I didn't want to go to the carnival with Riley either. People would start to notice Jordy missing. In fact, I was amazed the other two men hadn't already reported his murder, if not to the police, then to Bulldog Mackenzie. I wouldn't have been at all surprised if a gang of the carny guys were laying in wait for me.

Riley pulled over the bike, and the engine died. I climbed off the back, my heart dipping at the space my movement had created between us.

"Well, thanks," I said, glancing at the ground, shuffling my feet. Did 'thanks' cover it when someone helped you cover up a murder?

Riley swung his leg over the seat, to stand beside me.

"What are you doing?" I asked.

"Taking you back to your room. What do you think?"

"I can get back to my room just fine."

"Crap. You've been through a trauma. You're not fine, even if you keep pretending you are."

How could I tell him I wasn't fine, but for all the wrong reasons? I'd proven to myself that I could lose control, and I worried now I'd unleashed the beast, it would be harder to rein back in when the urge took hold. What if Riley stimulated my bloodlust again, as he had in the past? What would happen if I hurt him? I would never forgive myself.

"Please, Riley. Just let me go."

"No. I'm not letting you be on your own right now."

"My roommate, Brooke, will probably be there. I won't be on my own."

He frowned. "Brooke? As in Brooke Squires?"

"Yeah," I said, my unease deepening. "Why?"

"Then I'm definitely not letting you back to your room on your own." He took me by the hand and started to head toward my building, half-pulling me with him. This time I let him, my mind too jumbled with thoughts to protest. What about Brooke? Was her denial about what I'd seen, and her disappearance the night before, nothing to do with blocking out her memory, and everything to do with her lying her ass off?

Something else occurred to me. "Hey, how did you know something had happened with me? Did the other two guys tell you?"

"They came back, and I overheard them talking. They seemed scared, but they wouldn't admit why. I knew something had happened."

We snuck into the building. Most people would be sleeping, but the chance a couple of students would be hanging out remained. We moved quickly, taking the stairs, me running almost silently on my bare feet. Riley followed me, though he knew where my room was—after all, he'd been there before.

I reached my floor and ran down the corridor toward my room. The door was closed so I pushed it open. The room was in darkness, though moonlight slanted through the window, offering enough light to see. I frowned at Brooke's bed. The bedcovers lay flat, the pillow still plumped. No one had slept in that bed tonight.

"She's not here," I hissed to Riley, lurking outside the door.

He stepped through and shut the door behind him. "Good."

I could barely believe Riley was in my room again, only this time he'd been invited. My breath was shallow with nerves, and I fiddled anxiously with the cuffs on his jacket. I had no idea what I was supposed to do with him now.

"You'll need your jacket back," I said, simply trying to fill the silence between us. But then I realized that doing so would involve me taking it off, which would once again mean I'd have to stand, almost naked, in front of him.

He moved forward, closing the gap between us, and caught me by the shoulders. "Hey, it's okay."

"What do you mean?"

"You don't need to be nervous around me. I'm not going to do anything you don't want me to."

"I'm not nervous," I blustered. I didn't want him to know he was getting to me. He reached out and caught the collar of his jacket, using it to tug me forward slightly. He looked down at me, his hair falling forward, his hands still on the lapels so I could feel the warmth of him melting through to my collar bone. The expression in his eyes was intense and unmistakable.

He was going to kiss me. My first real kiss. My world spun, like a tornado encased us while we stood at its center. He leaned into me and his lips met mine, soft and warm, and instantly my mouth opened to him, our tongues meeting.

Fire raced through me, and I experienced a surge of desire. I was lost in him. I'd never felt this way around anyone before, like he recognized me so completely, like he knew me before we'd even spoken to one another. His hands moved from the lapels, to the zipper at my throat, and he slowly lowered the zipper. The rasp filled the room. My arms had found their way around his neck, and I arched myself into him, pressing my breasts against his chest. Only his t-shirt was in the way of our skin touching. His hands ran down, slipping beneath the back of the jacket, his palms cupping my panty-clad buttocks, to press me against him. I was breathing hard, our passion intensifying. I didn't want to break this moment, but I felt as though I was losing control. I was frightened of what happened when I lost control.

I broke the kiss, moving away.

"I can't," I stuttered. I didn't want him to think badly of me, or think of me as immature or a tease, but I needed to stay true to myself. "We can't … It's too soon."

He took my rejection graciously, though I could see the disappointment on his face. "Of course. Whatever you want."

He went to my dresser and pulled open a couple of drawers, before pulling out an oversized, white and blue, Los Angeles Dodgers t-shirt. I clutched his jacket closed with my fist at my sternum, but he removed my hand and slid the jacket from my shoulders. He pulled the top over my head, covering my body, and then kissed me on the nose.

"There. I can't say I've ever made a girl wear more clothing before, but you're worth waiting for."

I smiled, while my insides twisted with jealousy at the idea of him undressing another girl. I hoped he wouldn't think I was a total prude. I didn't want his nickname for me taking on a whole new slant. But I was still a virgin, and while I hadn't exactly been holding onto my virginity, or guarding it like something sacred, I still didn't want the day I lost my virginity to be forever tied in my mind with the day I'd killed a man.

But if I was going to lose it to anyone, I would want it to be Riley.

"I don't want you to go," I admitted.

"I don't want to go."

"Will you lay with me a while?"

A smile tugged his perfect mouth, a mouth I'd been kissing only moments before. "Of course."

I climbed into bed, and he got in after me, still wearing his jeans and t-shirt, though he kicked off his boots. He held out his arms to me, and I snuggled down into him. His arms enveloped me. My cheek pressed against his chest, my arm slung over his body, and my thigh hooked over his jean-clad leg. He ran his fingertips lightly along the length of my arm, up and down.

Riley stopped, and I felt him shift slightly as he looked down.

He held my arm by the wrist and lifted it up.

"What are these?" he said, pointing at the series of raised scarred lines across my skin.

I snatched my arm away. I'd allowed my defenses down for a moment and I'd been caught. "Nothing."

"Don't give me that. I'm not stupid."

"Then you know what they are," I muttered, my cheeks flaring hot with shame. My body had stiffened, my arm drawn back into my body, but he reached out and pulled me back into the position we'd been in before, and kissed the top of my head.

"You should never hurt yourself, Icy. Why would you do this?"

His fingertips lightly traced the fading scars on my forearm. For once, I made no attempt to pull away or cover the scars up.

I answered his question with a question. "Why do you put yourself in danger by riding upside down on a motorbike at God-knows what speed?"

"It vents my frustrations," he said, a half-smile playing on his lips.

"Then I guess we do harmful things for exactly the same reason."

"You vent your frustration at something?"

I wanted to tell him then, tell him exactly what I was and the problems I struggled with. The words danced on my tongue, desperate to burst from my lips. But I couldn't do it. I couldn't stand to see the horror in his eyes, and to have him push me away and run from the room.

He must know something is different about you, a little voice spoke in my head. *You ripped the throat out of a grown man who was three times your size. He knows a normal girl wouldn't be able to do such a thing.*

So why hadn't he asked me? Why hadn't he even mentioned what I did?

CHAPTER 16

NO DREAMS CAME to me that night.

I knew without opening my eyes that Riley was no longer beside me. I didn't blame him for leaving, though that didn't change the pang of longing inside me, or the dip of disappointment in the pit of my stomach. I understood he would want to slip off campus under the cover of darkness.

Just as I instinctively knew Riley was gone, I also sensed Brooke was back in her bed. Did she know where she'd been the previous night? Had she been to a party, or had she been doing something far more odious?

I'd woken more refreshed than I'd done for ages. Was my clear head down to the lack of dreams, or perhaps the blood I'd consumed the previous night, or even Riley? I thought all three things were intimately connected, that one would not have happened without the other, so I guessed it was probably all three.

My emotions were torn. I'd killed a man last night—a horrific and unthinkable thing to do. And yet, here I was, encased within a happy little bubble that was Riley. The scent of him on my bedclothes, in my hair, on my skin. I hugged myself with happiness.

Still, it was madness, surely, to be filled with such crazy joy at the simple thought of a boy—a dark, strange, possibly dangerous boy—when I had become a killer myself.

I needed to get to class, though I wondered how I would ever concentrate on lectures with so many thoughts and questions going through my head. Riley had not had the chance to explain his reaction to Brooke's name last night, but I was sure she was connected to whatever was going down in Sage Springs. Plus, Flynn knew something about the pools, which made me think he was also involved. Why had he taken me there in the first place? Had he been trying to tell me something, show me something, perhaps, but then had been scared off by the reaction of the pools? How could a body of water even respond to something a person said or even thought? It was crazy to think such a thing was a possibility, but I'd felt something when I'd been pushing Jordy's body beneath the glass-like surface. Something … else.

It all revolved around the pools. Whatever was building in town was going to culminate there, and I was sure both Brooke and Flynn were involved, together with the carny guys. I just wished I had the inkling of an idea about what it was exactly. I wasn't used to not knowing things.

There was only one person I'd met who, apart from when I'd managed to upset her, I'd gotten no bad vibes from. I wasn't sure she'd even talk to me, but she'd recognized the necklace, and I was certain she knew the symbol, the same symbol I'd seen drawn on Brooke's body. I had questions and I needed answers.

Leaving Brooke huddled beneath the covers of her bed, I grabbed my wash bag and clothes, took a quick shower, and headed to class. I kept my head down, but my eyes peeled for anything suspicious. I half expected the police to reappear, slap cuffs around my wrists, and arrest me for the murder of Jordy *Whateverhisnamewas*.

But everyone acted as if the world had continued as normal while mine had tilted so far on its axis I worried I would fall off.

Laurel wasn't in my first class, but I caught sight of her hurrying down the corridor between classes, her dark hair falling from the twist she wore as she pushed her glasses higher up her nose.

"Laurel!" I called.

She hesitated, but didn't stop walking. It was the tiniest motion, but enough for me to know she'd heard me. My heart dropped with sadness. I'd hoped we'd be able to be friends, but she didn't even want to talk to me. I couldn't say I blamed her.

Even though she didn't want to talk to me, that didn't mean I still didn't need to talk to her.

"Laurel!" I called again, louder this time, causing other students to glance my way. I took after her, pushing past people, ignoring their mocking stares. "Hey, Laurel. Wait up a minute."

She glanced over her shoulder and slowed with a resigned sigh. "I can't talk. I'm busy."

"Please. Just a few minutes. I'm sorry if things I've done have made you pissed at me, but this is really important."

She shook her head. "Sorry, I can't. I've been told ..."

Laurel slammed her mouth shut and abruptly turned from me and started to walk again.

I stared after her retreating back. "Told what?"

No way was I going to give up this easily. I chased after her, grabbed her arm and pulled her back around. "Told what?" I repeated.

She glared at me. "Told not to speak to you."

Something caught my eye. Where her sleeve had ridden up, on her inner wrist was the tattoo of the same symbol—the circle with a star in the middle—that seemed to be haunting me.

"Right," I said, resolutely. "You're going to answer some questions, whether you like it or not."

"What about class?"

"Screw class. We'll call this a study break."

I kept my hand on her arm. My strength meant she wouldn't be able to break free. With my head down, I marched her down the hall, out of the building, and toward my car.

Feeling a little brutal, but at my wits' end, I opened the passenger door and pushed her in. Laurel didn't fight back, which surprised me. Did she feel the need to talk as much as I did? Perhaps this was her way of telling whoever was lording it over her that she'd been forced into a conversation.

I walked around the other side and climbed in behind the wheel before twisting to face her. "Right. Spill it. Something bad is going to happen in town, and I know it's connected with that symbol you have tattooed on your wrist. And who the hell told you not to speak to me?"

Sarcasm filled her response. "Enough questions, already?"

I had managed to cram in a few. "Okay, first thing first, who told you not to speak to me?"

She glanced away as though embarrassed she'd allowed someone else to tell her what to do. "The rest of my circle. They know there's something different about you. They just can't pinpoint exactly what."

"Circle? Like circle of friends?" I wasn't sure she had that many.

But she shook her head and lifted her eyes, focusing on me. "No, circle of witches. Like a coven."

"Witches?"

She shrugged. "I don't expect you to believe me, but you asked what was going on, so I've told you. Do what you want with it."

I thought back to the conversation I'd had with Flynn about how all the names of the places in Sage Springs were linked to the town's history, and how the founders of the town had all been into their herbal medicine. I already knew magic was involved here, from the symbols, to the pools, to the dreams I'd been having since I got here. The existence of a coven didn't surprise me, though Laurel's involvement did.

"I believe you. Is that what the symbol is for, the one with the star and the circle? Magic?"

"Yes. We are the points of the star, and the circle binds us. We're all descendents of the original founders of the town, and it's our job to watch over Sage Springs. Make sure it stays safe."

"But it isn't going to stay safe," I said, my tone suddenly urgent. "Something bad is going to happen."

She narrowed her eyes. "How do you know that? Is it like how you knew about the accident at the carnival? I told you the truth, now it's your turn."

The truth, the whole truth, and nothing but the truth. I pondered the idea for a moment and decided against it. The partial truth would have to do.

"I see things that haven't happened yet," I admitted. "And some things that have happened already."

"Wow. You're a precog?"

"A what?"

"A precognitive. Someone who can see the future."

"Well, yeah. I guess that's what I am then." I wasn't planning on filling her in on the 'and I'm half vampire' part.

"And you think something bad is going to happen?"

I nodded. "I know it is. I've been seeing it ever since I got here."

She chewed on her lower lip.

"What is it?" I asked.

"I don't know if it's connected, but in about eighteen hours there will be a Disruptive Convergence."

"A what?"

"There will be an exceptional alignment of planets in our solar system. The moon and three other planets will be aligned in such a way that it will cause a great shift in the earth's energy from one of peace to war."

I couldn't help my laugh of disbelief. "This is supposed to be a peaceful world?"

"Yes, compared to what the world would be like in a warlike cycle. The way the planets align mean that the earth's dark energies can be tapped into. This isn't just a warlike cycle, it's also known as the 'hell' cycle."

"That doesn't sound good."

"You can say that again."

"But why Sage Springs?"

"There's a place in the forest that's special—"

"The pools," I interrupted. "I've seen them."

Laurel widened her eyes at me. "You have?"

"Yeah, a couple of times now."

"Oh… kay," she said slowly, as if taking this new piece of information in. "Well, the pools in the forest act as portals between our world and the afterlife. Flynn is supposed to protect them, but since the mining has come so close, he's struggled."

"Flynn?" I said. "Why Flynn?"

"Flynn Matthews is an Elemental."

"A what?" I was starting to feel like a parrot squawking out the same two words over and over.

"An Elemental," she restated. "They're powerful witches who can control the elements."

"You've got to be kidding." I'd come across witchcraft before, but not this particular kind. Trust my luck to have decided to make my home in a town full of god-damned witches. "So can he control all elements?" The thought of this was so powerful, it was terrifying.

But Laurel shook her head. "No. Each Elemental has a specific element they can control. For Flynn, it's water."

"Which is why he's such a strong swimmer," I said, piecing things together.

"That definitely helps. But when the planets align, they have an effect on the water—"

"Like the moon and the tide?" I offered.

She smiled. "Exactly. So the water is displaced, and this makes it easier for the afterlife to pass through into our world."

Was that where the body had ended up, I wondered, together with my clothes? In the afterlife? Riley had said that things didn't come back once they'd entered the pools, but what if they did? What if at a particular time, when the planets were aligned, they were able to come back?

I didn't mention either Jordy's body or my bloodied clothes to Laurel. Instead, I said, "And this is what creates the hell cycle?"

She nodded, but this time her expression was grim. "Yep. The hell cycle."

"But what have the carnival people got to do with all of this?"

"We're not totally sure. They come here every year, do their thing, and move on. Plenty of people in town have a thing against them, 'cause they think they're a godless lot, and bring crime and violence into Sage Springs. But the truth is that they've never really caused much trouble." She shrugged. "Thing is, we can't ignore that they've stayed now, just when the Convergence is about to happen."

We stared at each other, neither of us having an answer to this particular question.

"You need to come and speak to the rest of my circle," Laurel said. "Can you come to my house, tonight? Say about seven? I can't tell you where we meet, but I can take you there."

I nodded. "Okay, I'll be there."

Laurel pulled a piece of paper from her purse and scribbled down her address. "I'll tell the others you're coming, and you're not what they think."

I frowned. "What do they think?"

"That you are something different. Something dark."

A shiver ran through me, but I tried to hide it. They'd not been far wrong. What would they do if they found out the truth?

"I'm no danger to you or your circle," I said, truthfully.

"I'll tell them," she said with a small smile. She opened the door and climbed from the car. "I'll see you later."

"Sure."

I wondered who made up the rest of the circle. I guessed the photographer, Melissa, due to me finding her necklace, but I was at a loss about the rest. How many would there be and how powerful were they? I worried that as soon as I walked into their meeting place they would use a spell to find out exactly what I was. But if they were able to conduct such a spell, wouldn't they have done so already?

More than anything else, I wanted to see Riley again. What would he tell me to do? I guessed he'd advise me to stay away from a group of witches who might turn on me if they found out I was half-vampire. But then Riley didn't know I was half-vampire, though he must realize there's plenty not normal about me.

The ring of my cell phone made me jump. I scrabbled around in my bag to find it. I was amazed it was still charged. No one ever called me, except my mom, and I experienced a pang of guilt that I'd not called them yesterday. I knew both my parents would be worrying.

Glancing at the screen, I didn't recognize the number.

I hit the answer button. "Hello?"

"Ms. Bandores?"

"Yes?"

"This is the garage working on your car. I'm calling to let you know it will be ready for collection this afternoon."

"Already? I thought it would be at least another few days?"

I could almost hear the shrug. "Well, it's ready now. Parts came in early. So are you going to come collect it, or not?"

"Yes, of course I am. I'll be there this afternoon."

I hung up and reached out to pat the dashboard of the old SUV. I'd grown fond of the old car, and didn't want the conspicuousness of my brand new Audi. I was having a hard enough time not getting myself noticed around here, and my L.A. wheels wouldn't help any.

Leaving the car, I slunk back to class. I was massively late, and attracted the glare of my lecturer as I slipped into a seat near the back and fired up my laptop.

Suddenly, my hearing went strange, as if I'd been submerged under water. I reached out and grabbed the edges of my laptop, as if that would somehow secure me to reality. But the machine felt slippery beneath my touch, and I couldn't get a proper hold on it. I groaned, knowing something was coming that I didn't want to see. On stage, my professor continued his talk, pointing to things on the interactive white board, but I couldn't focus on what he was saying. I could barely hear him. A rushing sound raced past my ears, like waves or the wind. Before my eyes, a liquid black began to steal in from all sides of the white board, rapidly creeping and crawling down until all of the writing was gone, and I stared only at a black square. It spilled from the wall and flooded across the stage, slipping up the professor's legs. He looked down, as if only just noticing what was happening, and began to scream. It crept up his body, crawling over him like a living thing. More of the darkness slid down toward the students sitting in the front rows. Their screams filled the lecture hall, as they turned in their seats to climb over one another to try to get away. The wave of students clambered in panic toward where I still sat, frozen, at the back.

It would claim them, this darkness. I knew it. Whatever was beneath the water in the pools was powerful, and it would take their souls as its own.

My ears popped, and I found myself back in the normal lecture hall. I must have made a noise, as a couple of students turned their heads toward me. I ducked down, hiding behind the screen of my laptop.

Danger felt so close this time. The premonitions were getting stronger, and I could only assume that was because the event itself was also getting closer. Laurel had said this aligning of the planets—what had she called it, a Disruptive Convergence—would happen in a matter of hours, not days.

My thoughts went back to the dreams I'd had, of the people of Sage Springs empty and lost, of the town in darkness. I didn't think the darkness I'd just seen was a literal interpretation of what was going to happen, and neither was the stream of empty people heading into the woods. My foresight gave me interpretations of what was going to happen. It wasn't like watching the actual event on a television screen, unless it was connected to an actual person, and then it tended to be more accurate. But I'd never seen something this big before. I wasn't someone who predicted airline disasters, or train wrecks. If I was, perhaps I'd have been able to make a difference to this god-forsaken world a little sooner. All I could interpret was that something dark was coming to Sage Springs, and I had a theory that it would feed on the souls of the inhabitants.

I couldn't believe that this happening was a natural occurrence. Something other than the Convergence was at play here. I just had to figure out what and who.

The carnival people. It had to be them.

But did that mean Riley was involved as well?

CHAPTER 17

I WENT TO collect my car with dread in my heart.

Something terrible was going to happen in Sage Springs, and I had no idea how to stop it.

The garage was located a couple of miles from the outskirts of town. The rental company was there to meet me, and quickly checked off the SUV. I handed over the keys and gave the old girl a hearty slap, like a faithful horse, as I did so. My scribble on a piece of paper completed the receipt.

I walked into the garage. My car waited for me at the front, but no one else seemed to be around. Heading deeper into the cave of the garage, a set of feet protruded from beneath a station wagon that had been raised from the floor using a couple of jacks. I wondered why they'd not used the raising platform fixed to the interior of the garage to check beneath the car. Perhaps it was broken.

"Hello?" I called again.

A grunt responded, and the feet began to move with a shuffle and a scrape. Had he been sleeping under there?

The mechanic hauled himself out from beneath the car. Dark patches of sweat stains, yellow and old, marked beneath the arms of his t-shirt and around his neck. He was at least a hundred pounds overweight. I was surprised he hadn't gotten himself wedged under the vehicle.

"Hi. I'm here to collect the Audi."

He looked me up and down. I could sense the sneer on his face, though he managed to repress it. I didn't need to be psychic to know exactly what he was thinking—spoilt little rich girl come to collect the big car mommy and daddy paid for. The worst thing was that he wasn't far wrong.

"I got a call this morning to say it was ready."

He snorted and wiped the back of his hand beneath his nose. I tried not to grimace. "That's right." His eyes narrowed at me. "Need you to sign some paperwork and then car's all yours."

"I thought the repairs would take longer than it did."

"Parts came through fast, that's all," he snapped.

"Right."

Jeez, I hope he didn't treat every customer with such disdain, or I figured he'd go out of business pretty quick. He seemed like one of those guys who would never take anyone of the female persuasion seriously.

He pushed a couple of forms under my nose, which I signed, and then he slid my keys across the counter. I snatched them up, grateful to be out of there. I didn't want to spend any more time in the guy's presence.

I climbed inside my car, sliding into the soft leather. The familiar scent and feel of the vehicle caused a wave of homesickness to sweep over me. I bit my lower lip, glancing down to stare at the steering wheel to compose myself. I couldn't run off home. Not now. I hadn't been raised to be a coward, and how could I go back to Los Angeles, abandoning everyone in Sage Springs to face whatever horror was coming?

I reached down to the ignition and turned the key, the car purring to life around me. A sigh issued from deep within my lungs. I would meet with Laurel's circle tonight and see what happened. Maybe everything would change after that meeting. Still, my stomach churned with nerves. I had no way of predicting how that meeting would go.

It was only a couple of miles' drive back into town, heading down the windy road through the forest. A quick fiddle with the radio found a local station, and a pop song blasted out. Far too chirpy, bouncy, and generally enthusiastic for me. I reached out and flicked the radio off, the interior of the car falling back into silence, except for the purr of the engine.

The road curved around a bend. I put my foot on the brake to slow, but nothing happened. Alarm spiked through me. I jammed my foot down harder—a movement that should have thrown the car into an emergency stop. Nothing happened.

"Shit!"

The curve approached, and I had no choice but to handle the vehicle so it hugged the road. My heart thumped hard and fast, climbing up into my throat, my breath shallow. I forced myself to focus, to not panic, but my mind blurred with fear. How would I stop with no brakes? A thousand pieces of advice I'd picked up on subconsciously over the last year ran through my mind: turn into a skid, stay calm if you get stranded, try to minimize impact. I had no idea which piece of this information was any use to me now. I could hardly minimize impact, could I?

The Audi gathered momentum created by the downward incline of the road.

Another car headed toward me in the opposite lane. I caught sight of the family inside, the father's brow furrowed as he passed, clearly thinking I was going too fast, but with no idea why. I stared back at him in fear, wanting to shout for help but knowing it would do no good. How could anyone help me?

I was thankful I'd managed to keep control so far, but the closer to town I got, the more vehicles and people would be around. I couldn't risk getting that close. I healed quickly, but a regular person wouldn't. Though this wasn't my fault, if I mowed down a family, I would never forgive myself.

I needed to stop the car.

I cast a quick glance at the handbrake. What would happen if I pulled it on? I worried it would make a bad situation worse, and throw the car into an uncontrollable skid, but I didn't know what else to do, and I didn't have the luxury of time to ponder on it. The road tore by, my fingers wrapped tight around the steering wheel, my knuckles white. I needed to do something right now or I would be risking other lives as well as my own.

The ignition, I suddenly thought. If I turned off the ignition, and then pulled on the handbrake, surely the car would have to slow down? A bank of trees and bushes ran alongside me. While I didn't want to wrap my car around a tree, I needed to bring it to a halt.

"Oh, hell." My voice was a whine of despair.

Gritting my teeth, I took one hand off the wheel and turned off the ignition. Power died from the car. Then I yanked up the handbrake.

The powerful car's back wheels locked. I heard the screeching of rubber on asphalt, and the stench of chemicals burning filled the interior. Smoke poured from the back. The steering wheel wrenched from my grip as the car skidded to one side, and I fought to keep it under control. The front end swung toward the undergrowth.

The hood buffeted through the bushes, leaves and twigs smashing and flying into the windshield.

Instinctively, I threw up my arms to protect my face.

The car bumped and jerked and bounced, my teeth snapping together, bones jarring. It hit something, and my body snapped forward, the seat belt slamming across my chest. My head flew forward, though I'd managed to tuck my chin to my chest, so my forehead hit the steering column, rather than breaking my nose or teeth, before the belt snapped me back again. Even so, pain shattered through my head and across my chest. I had a moment of consciousness to wonder if either my ribs or skull had been broken, and why my airbags didn't deploy. Had someone at the garage deactivated them?

But the car had come to a standstill. I drifted into a welcome black for the briefest of moments, but shook myself out of it. I couldn't lose consciousness. There might be a fuel leak, and I didn't want to end up burning to death while I was unconscious. I didn't think even a half-vampire could come back from that.

With a groan, my fingers scrambled to unclick my seat belt. I tried to open my door, but metal banged against wood. The door was jammed against a tree trunk on the other side. Wearily, I turned my sore head to the passenger door. The distance between here and there felt like a chasm.

I had to do it. I couldn't stay trapped inside the car in the hope someone came along. I checked for my purse, thinking I could get my phone and call for help, but it was nowhere to be seen. The bag had probably been flung to the back of the car, or was wedged under the seat. If I struggled to believe I could make it across one seat, there was no way I could search the inside of the vehicle.

Digging deep, I searched for my inner strength.

You heal quickly, I told myself. *You'll start feeling stronger really soon.*

As if my reassurance had a physical effect, the pain in my head and ribs began to lessen. I'd not been able to take a deep breath due to the pain, but was now able to, the inrush of oxygen helping to clear my head.

Okay, I could do this. It was only a matter of a couple of feet, and then I would be out of here.

Carefully, I reached over to hook my fingers around the dashboard. Using the strength in my legs, I lifted myself up to scoot over the handbrake and stick shift. Legs trembling, the stick shift jabbing me in the back of my thighs, I plopped into the passenger seat. I sat, panting, while I got my strength back again. Such a simple movement had drained every ounce out of me.

A sudden wind buffeted the car, sending it rocking. I let out a scream, clinging to the sides of my seat. The idea that I'd somehow found myself on the edge of a cliff, and that the wind would tip the car over, sprang into my head, but my overactive imagination was working, rather than a premonition of any kind. I rarely saw anything about myself directly. For once, I hated that fact. Perhaps if I had, I would have known something was wrong with the car and refused to take it. One thing I was certain of was that the car had been tampered with on purpose. Someone wanted me dead, and I thought Bulldog Mackenzie and his crew were the most likely cause. They knew what I'd done to Jordy and had taken their revenge. I had no idea if the unpleasant guy at the garage knew what was wrong with the car, if he'd been in on it. Then I got a flash of a young man tied up out back, rocking in a wooden chair he was bound to, yelling against the gag wrapped around his mouth.

Damn it. The horrible guy hadn't even been a mechanic. He was one of the carny guys.

That explained why he hadn't been using the proper equipment in the garage when I'd arrived. He'd just been playing the part. How did they think they'd get away with this?

But I knew how. I wouldn't be able to report them without coming up with a reason why they'd want me dead, and that I'd killed one of their own was hardly something I would ever go to the cops about. They'd keep the young garage attendee quiet with a few simple threats of bodily harm.

A hand slammed against the outside of the passenger widow, and I let out a scream, my heart rate jumping, my hand clutched to my chest.

A face lowered down to the glass, and I sighed with relief and sagged back into my seat.

Riley!

He cracked open the door. "What the hell, Icy? What happened?"

I stifled a sob and fell into his arms, my arms wrapping around the back of his neck, my face pressing against the side of his throat.

"Hey," he said, stroking my hair. "You're okay now. Everything is okay."

I allowed myself the luxury of him holding me for a few moments while I got myself together. I had to admit, the feel of his skin beneath my nose and mouth brought me a comfort I could never have even imagined before I met him. I wanted to close my eyes and lose myself in his skin, forget about the hellish event due to happen only hours from now, and that someone wanted me dead.

Sitting back up, I sniffed and brushed my hair from my face. He reached out and gently touched the wound on my forehead. I winced at the contact.

"Sorry," he said. "Did you just do that? It looks like it's healing already."

"Yeah, I heal fast." I didn't know a lie that would work.

He cocked his eyebrows in surprise. "You sure do." He pressed his lips together. "So what the hell happened, Icy? You in a habit of getting yourself into dangerous situations?"

I gave a cold laugh. "Yeah. I guess I am. Something went wrong with the brakes on my car. I had to stop it so I switched off the engine, pulled on the handbrake, and rammed the car into a bush."

"Jesus!"

I hesitated, wanting to tell him I thought Bulldog Mackenzie and the others were involved, but I kept my mouth shut. I wanted to trust Riley. After all, he'd helped me hide a body, but I struggled to trust anyone fully. Life had already taught me trust shouldn't be given away lightly.

"I guess the lightning strike fried more than the electronics."

"Sure did." His beautiful face contorted with anger. "The damn mechanic should have checked the whole car over!"

I put a hand on his arm. "It's fine, Riley. I'm fine."

"No, you're not. I should get you to a hospital."

"Honestly, it looks worse than it is. It's the shock, that's all." I could feel the skin on my forehead, tightening, itching, as it healed. Within a few days, the cut would be almost invisible, just the white line of a scar remaining. I wasn't sure how I would explain that to Riley, but if the whole hell cycle thing happened, I imagined it would be the least of my worries.

"Please, Riley. I don't want to go to the police, hospital, or anywhere else that involves the authorities. No one was hurt, thank God. Can we just go home?"

Except, I didn't know where home was for me. Not anymore.

CHAPTER 18

RILEY STARED AT me intently, his normally full mouth a serious line, before nodding. "Okay," he relented, "but I'm not taking you back to your dorm to be on your own, and I can't sneak in with you at this time of day. You're coming back with me."

My heart rate stepped up a notch at the idea of being back on the midway. "No." I shook my head. "I don't want anyone to see me."

"They won't. I'll sneak you in the back. Most people won't be around this time of day anyway. We tend to be night owls."

My stomach churned with nerves at the thought of being so close to the people who I believed wanted me dead, but my desire to be with Riley was stronger than my fear.

"You promise you can get me in without being seen?"

He lifted his hand, his little finger cocked in front of my face. "Pinky promise," he said with a grin.

I reached out and hooked my little finger around his. Even such a tiny contact sent shivers of desire racing through me. I wanted to take off his skin and climb inside his body with him, immerse myself fully, blend until we were like one being.

We grinned at each other, our pinkies locked, and I completely forgot the pains in my body and the fact someone wanted to kill me.

Riley leaned forward and kissed the top of my head. The hand our fingers had been joined at moved into a fuller grip, and he helped me stand from the car. His other arm slipped around my waist, supporting me. I figured I could probably walk just fine on my own, but I wasn't going to give him an excuse to move away.

We stepped back from the car, and I gasped. My head spun. The whole of the hood was crumpled like an accordion. A spider web of cracks ran through the windscreen, the wing mirror completely knocked off on the driver's side. The seriousness of what had happened hit me. I was lucky to be alive. I was lucky I hadn't crashed into another car, or hit a pedestrian.

"My God," I breathed.

"See why I was so worried?"

I nodded. I couldn't deal with the car right now. I'd need to call a tow truck again, even go to the police and tell them I'd had an accident—someone was bound to spot the wreckage at some point and report it—but I didn't have the head space. The cops would almost certainly come looking for me at school again. At least at Riley's I would be safe from the police asking me more questions.

"Let's just get out of here."

With our bodies slotted together, we stepped out of the forest, and back onto the road. Riley's bike sat parked on the curb. His helmet hung from the handle bar. I'd never seen him wear it before. I wondered why he'd brought it this time.

"Here," he said, taking the helmet off the handlebar and handing it to me.

"What about you?"

He shrugged. "I don't need it. You're the one with the head injury."

"But—" I started to protest, but he silenced me with a lift of his hand.

"Wear it, Icy, or you're not coming on the bike."

I sighed, but lifted the helmet and carefully slid it over my face, wincing as it made contact with my sore forehead. Riley had already climbed on the bike, so I swung my leg over the back of the seat and climbed on behind him. Automatically, I wrapped my hands around his waist, no longer worrying about the space between us or if I should hold onto the seat.

The bike roared beneath me, and Riley pulled away from the curb, heading in the same direction my car had been going. He crossed town, staying on the outskirts so he didn't head right through Main Street. We got a few glances from people, but no one knew who I was with the helmet on.

Riley stayed on the coastal road until he was past the carnival, still and silent, and under investigation, then he doubled back on himself. He took a small road that led to the beach, and cut back up so he was at the back of the carnival where the carnies' trailers were parked. As he'd predicted, there didn't seem to be many people around.

Still some distance from his trailer, he cut the power from the bike. "Keep the helmet on," he told me. "Just in case someone is being nosy."

He dragged the bike toward his trailer, and I hurried alongside him. He left the bike at the back of his home, and quickly ran up the steps to unlock the trailer. I noticed this time he'd locked the front door.

I was relieved to be inside Riley's home again. Carefully, I pulled the helmet off and shook out my hair. Riley stepped in front of me, took the helmet from my hands and set it down on the small, fold out table. He straightened and reached out to me with both hands. His fingers lightly touched my temples, and he tilted my head slightly. His thumb brushed the cut as he inspected it.

"It really does seem better," he noted.

"It's fine." I thought of something. "How did you find me, anyway?"

"I happened to be riding out on that road. It's good for bikes. I spotted your car from the road."

"Really? But it seemed almost hidden by the bushes."

"Nah, I'm observant, that's all."

"Riding on a motorbike at god-knows how many miles per hour?"

He laughed and lowered his forehead to mine. "What are you saying, Icy? Are you worried I'm stalking you?"

I hadn't been, until then. "And yesterday?" I dared to say. "What about when you found me? How did you know then?"

"I told you, I overheard the guys talking after they got back here. They gave a vague direction. I just followed it and got lucky."

I wasn't sure you could call finding me with a dead body and covered in blood lucky, but I didn't know what other explanation he could give.

"Don't doubt me, Icy," he said, but his voice was low, intense. "I've given you no reason to think I'm anything but helpful."

"Yeah, maybe a bit too helpful." Damn my mouth. Why couldn't I learn when to keep it shut?

"You need to let people in."

But I shook my head. "Not people," I said. "Only you."

We locked eyes, my breath growing shallower by the second. I was breathing him in, our faces a mere inch apart. His hands still cupped my cheeks, his fingers in my hair.

"Riley," I started, but I didn't know what I planned on saying. He wasn't listening anyway. He ducked his head a little, bringing his mouth closer to mine. My breath stopped in my chest, my lips tingling in anticipation. He placed his mouth against mine, and my eyes slipped shut. My entire being focused on that one point, the touch of his mouth on mine. The warmth of his lips, the slight opening of his mouth, the exact amount of pressure he applied.

My body acted of its own accord. My arms wound around his neck, my back arching to push my torso closer to his. He still wore his jacket, the leather soft and worn beneath my hands. He deepened the kiss and I responded, opening my mouth to him so our tongues did a slow, delicious dance.

Riley scooped me up. He was only a couple of inches taller than me, but he was strong and wiry. He pushed through the small trailer into the bedroom at the back and unceremoniously dumped me on the bed.

"Hey," I protested. "I'm injured, remember."

He glowered down at me, his black hair falling in his face. "Just stop talking."

I clamped my mouth shut as he shrugged his jacket from his shoulders and pulled his t-shirt over his head. My eyes absorbed the sight of him, the jeans riding low on his hips, exposing the jutted lines that marked his hip bones. A spatter of dark chest hair ran across his pectoral muscles, and a line followed down the column of his abs, to his navel, and then further, disappearing beneath his worn out jeans. He kicked off his boots, and then climbed onto the bed with me.

"You're losing this top, you know?" he said. His fingers slipped beneath the hem of my long sleeved t-shirt, grazing the skin of my flat stomach, causing goose bumps to erupt all over me.

He was lying with me, face to face, with no shirt on. I flattened my palm and reached out to touch him. I placed my hand on his warm shoulder, to run down his smooth, well-muscled arm, and then back up again. My hands found my way around to his back, feeling the sharp edge of his shoulder blades, the thick muscles either side of his spine, the dip at his lower back. Finally, I positioned my hand on his chest, right above his heart, feeling the steady beat of his life force beneath my palm.

He smiled at me, and his smile made my heart burst with happiness. "What are you doing?"

"Learning every inch of you."

He grinned wickedly. "There are plenty more inches to go." And he leaned back in and captured my mouth again, drawing me into another deep, forceful kiss. This time his hand slid further beneath my top. I'd never been so conscious of the position of another person's hand before. Our legs tangled together, our bodies melded. My lips felt bruised from the force of our kiss, my face hot, my breath leaving my body in frantic gasps. I could have kissed him this way for hours. Riley returned my passion with fervor of his own, one hand knotted in my hair, while the other roamed my body, learning its curves and dips in the same way I had learned his.

I knew he wanted me, I could feel his desire pressed hard against my hip.

But he broke the kiss, edging away from me just a fraction of an inch, separating what should never be separated. I had to stop myself moaning in disappointment.

He gazed down into my eyes, intense, smoldering. "Is this okay, Icy? Is this what you want?"

Emotions welled up inside me. I nodded frantically. "Yes, more than anything else in the world."

And I did. I'd never been surer of anything. I belonged with Riley, and he belonged with me. I wanted to know his body as intimately as I knew my own. I wanted to be able to lay myself bare for him, and know, without doubt, that he would hold my heart with as much care and passion as he held my body.

I moved toward him this time, desperately wanting his mouth back on mine. I'd never experienced anything as wondrous as kissing Riley, and I doubted I would ever experience anything as intensely again.

He took me at my word. This time, when he reached down, he hooked his fingers beneath my top and slowly lifted it to expose my stomach and breasts. I shifted in the bed slightly, allowing him to pull the t-shirt over my head. He dropped it to the floor. Though I'd stood before Riley in just my panties before, even though I was still clad in my jeans and bra, this time was different. I wanted this. I knew how far I was going to go, and I was filled with nervous excitement. I was going to do it, finally, and not just with some low life I'd finally given in to, but with a guy I believed might be my soul mate.

We helped each other remove our jeans, struggling with the buttons and zippers, while still clinging to each other and doing our best not to stop kissing for a second. Riley's mouth left mine, but only for a moment, while he trailed kisses down my jaw and throat.

"We need to be safe," he murmured against my skin, before leaning across and yanking open a drawer in his bedside cabinet. He leaned back into me, holding a foil packet I instantly recognized but had no experience with.

Panic suddenly filled me. "I don't know what to do."

"Shush," he said, kissing me lightly on the lips, in teasing pecks, the kiss turning into a gentle bite on my lower lip that sent shivers through me. "Leave it up to me."

I wanted to touch him. Tentatively, I reached down, slipping my hand inside his shorts. He was solid iron, heated from within. Silky soft. As I tightened my grip on him, cautiously sliding my hand up and down his length, he let out a moan and dropped his head to my shoulder.

His hips moved in response to my strokes. "Oh, Icy," he groaned.

Riley lifted his head back up and we kissed again. His hand ran down my body, stopping to caress my breasts, his thumb grazing over my hardened nipple, before moving lower. I had to stop myself from holding my breath. His hand slipped inside my panties, delving down. His fingers sought the place no one else had ever been, and he slipped into my intimate heat. I gasped, my free hand gripping his shoulder, my other hand keeping up my rhythmical stroking of him.

I buried my face in his neck, and suddenly became aware of the thump of his pulse beneath his skin. Instantly, all my attention redirected toward that point, toward the thump of hot blood. My mouth ran dry, my throat closing over with a pang of pain. I licked my lips. No, I wouldn't let this ruin my first experience with a man. I fought the urge to bite him with every piece of strength I had.

I must have paused my movements, as Riley leaned back slightly to look at me, concern in his eyes.

"Is everything okay?"

I had a hold on this, I could control myself. I felt the bloodlust fading, the pain slipping away, and I nodded, then leaned in to kiss him again. "Don't stop," I told him.

I felt myself building as he touched me, a tight heat coiling at the very pit of my stomach. The rest of the world vanished, and I had the thought that at least if Bulldog Mackenzie had his way, I would have this moment of heaven to take with me into the next world.

I heard the rip of foil, and Riley lifted his hips to cast his shorts aside. He sheathed himself and then rolled my panties down my legs. He lifted himself between my thighs, spreading my legs before him.

"Are you sure?" he said, holding himself above me.

I didn't speak, but nodded and reached to the back of his head to pull him down to me for another kiss. I wrapped my heels around the backs of his thighs and lifted my hips to meet his.

He nudged against my most intimate place, pushing, meeting resistance at first.

"It's okay," I gasped, as I sensed him hesitate. "It's okay." And he pushed again, a little harder, breaching me. I cried out, but it was a pleasurable pain, like the pain of cutting, and we met each other with frantic thrusts, gripping each other's bodies.

Heat built inside me, pain and pleasure shattering my soul until I struggled to distinguish between the two. All thoughts of blood had vanished, and I was nothing more than an explosion of sensations that centered on the boy whose body surrounded me.

Afterward, we clung to each other, panting, Riley's body a heavy weight on mine. I didn't care. I would have held him like that until the last breath in my lungs had been crushed out of me.

Riley must have realized, because he lifted himself and slipped into the spot beside me on the bed. He gathered me to him, his arm around my shoulders, so my cheek rested on his chest. I put my arm around his waist and hugged him with pure, unbridled joy.

I had found my home, here in his arms. I didn't want to be anywhere else.

CHAPTER 19

THE LAST THING I wanted to do was leave Riley, but I needed to make my meeting with Laurel.

Thinking he was sleeping, I rolled away from him and began to climb from the bed. An arm snuck around my waist and pulled me back again. His mouth nuzzled my neck.

"Where do you think you're going?" he growled in my ear.

I placed my hand over the top of his and squeezed hard before letting go. "I've got to meet a friend. She'll be pissed if I'm late."

"Can I come?" he asked.

"No," I laughed. "It's girls only."

I wasn't actually sure if this was true, but I needed an excuse to keep Riley away. I had a feeling Laurel's circle would be even more furious with me if I turned up with Riley in tow. "I need to get back to my room first and get myself cleaned up." I hated the idea of washing the scent of him off my skin, but after the wreckage, and then spending the last couple of hours in Riley's bed, I figured I was a mess.

"Okay," he relented. "But you need to let me give you a ride back to campus."

I realized I didn't have any wheels of my own. I could walk, but that would make me late for sure. "I guess you'll have to."

He kissed my neck, sending shivers down me. "Your enthusiasm is overwhelming."

I twisted back around to face him, and kissed him on the mouth. "Sorry. I just worry about people gossiping." That was part of the truth.

"Screw them. Let them talk."

I smiled, but I didn't feel it. "Yeah, screw them."

We got up and got dressed, and within ten minutes I found myself on the back of Riley's bike, thundering down the road toward town. My position on the bike, with the powerful machine thrumming between my thighs, did nothing to help the ache down below that the last couple of hours with Riley had caused. I didn't mind. That I had something physical to remember what we'd done made me squeeze myself with joy. Within ten minutes, we approached campus. A group of students hung out beside one of the cars, another crowd sat on the grass in front of the building. They all turned and stared as the bike roared into the lot. I could feel everyone staring, whispering behind their hands to one another. I knew I shouldn't give a shit about what they were thinking or saying, I just wished I didn't.

"Thanks, Riley," I said, climbing off the bike. I pulled the helmet off and handed it back to him. Suddenly shy, I gave him a smile. "I'll see you later, yeah?"

Turning to walk away, I heard him say, "Hey, Icy!"

He reached out and caught my arm, tugging me back to him, before planting a kiss on my lips in front of everyone.

My cheeks flared with heat, but I couldn't help dissolving inside. He broke the kiss. "No more accidents, okay?"

I shook my head. "No more accidents," I agreed, though I had no idea what the next few hours might hold.

Riley tore away on his bike. Everyone got back to their own business. I thought I'd been forgotten until I glanced around and locked eyes with a familiar aqua stare.

Flynn was watching me. *Damn,* he must have seen me with Riley.

I lifted my hand in a half-wave, but he just turned and walked away.

My heart sank, though I wasn't sure why I even cared.

I only had half an hour before I needed to meet Laurel. Hurrying up to my room, I stood in front of the mirror and checked out the mark on my forehead. The wound still looked obvious and painful, but wasn't as red raw as it had been a few hours ago. I would be able to use a little makeup to try and disguise the injury. I showered and changed and was ready to head out again within fifteen minutes. I didn't have any wheels now, so I caught the bus into town and asked the driver to point me in the right direction of Laurel's home. The house was a beautiful, white clad property set back from the road. A porch ran right around, a swing to one side of the front door.

As I approached, the front door opened and Laurel appeared, facing in toward the house, shouting her goodbyes. "Yeah, I'll be back before eleven, Mom. Love you!"

She turned, pulling the door shut behind her as she did so. She caught sight of me and rolled her eyes back in the direction of her house. "My parents are over protective, you know?"

Then she got closer, and her eyes widened at the sight of my forehead. "Holy cow. What happened to you?"

Automatically, I reached up to touch the wound. "I fell up some steps," I lied. "Smacked my forehead on the top one."

"Wow. Too many drinks?"

I laughed. "If only. More like two left feet."

She seemed to buy my excuse. "So, are you ready to meet my circle?"

I shook my head. "Not really. I'm nervous, to be honest. It doesn't seem like they have a very good opinion of me."

"They don't understand you, that's all. We're used to knowing exactly who people are in the world, and you're something of an anomaly. When they find out you're nothing to fear, and that you want to help, I'm sure they'll warm up."

I hoped Laurel was right.

We headed down to the beach. Instead of staying on the natural C of the cove, Laurel headed northward, toward the cliff face that marked the end of the beach. I frowned, but stayed quiet and followed.

At first I thought she intended on climbing the rocky cliff, but then she turned to me with a secretive smile and nodded toward a craggy outcropping of rocks. "Do you see why I couldn't just tell you where to come?" Her smile was borderline smug.

I still wasn't sure what she was talking about, but another few footsteps, and a clamber on some slippery rocks, took me around the outcropping. A small natural archway was created in the cliff face, but followed the precipice around a bend so the gap wasn't naturally visible.

I entered the rock, the temperature instantly dropping. The small tunnel was low, causing me to duck, and I reached out to protect my already injured head from any more knocks. Within a minute, I stepped into the open air again.

I found myself standing on a small, hidden cove on a different part of the beach. A bonfire burned, candles lit around it. The waves rushed onto shore, a rhythmical, peaceful shush of millions of grains of sand moving at once.

Three figures sat around the bonfire, surrounded by candles. The power of the sun had lessened, but it wasn't yet dusk—that moment between day ending and dark falling. As I'd expected, Melissa was one of the three. The other two, though, I hadn't been prepared for. One of the other figures was Kayla, Brooke's friend. And the final one had a familiar halo of red curls.

"Dana?"

For some reason, she'd been the last person I'd expected to see here. She was one of the few people who'd been nice to me since I'd come to Sage Springs. But then I remembered when Melissa had collapsed at the dance, how Dana had been one of the people to rush in and help. I remembered how she'd kept pushing me toward Flynn, though I'd assumed it was because of the paper, not, I guessed, because she'd wanted Flynn to keep an eye on me.

Dana got to her feet as we approached, her expression neutral. Melissa and Kayla also stood, both facing me, their arms folded.

"Dana," I said again. "I had no idea."

"I wouldn't expect you to," she replied. "We're very careful about who knows about us."

"But…" I didn't know how to say what I wanted without sounding totally pathetic. What the hell. Being pathetic was probably the least of my worries. "But you always seemed to like me."

"I didn't know what you were, at first. But after the incident at the carnival, and you being in possession of Melissa's necklace, I started to see an aura around you. It's not good, Beth. Your aura is red, or at least it was a few days ago." Her eyes narrowed. "Right now, it's black."

I wanted to reach out and swipe my fingers through the cloud of color Dana claimed she saw around me. The reason for the change was clear to me. I had killed Jordy and fed from him. Perhaps it would go back to red eventually, but I wasn't even sure if red was any good.

"Beth, black indicates an absence of life. Clearly, you're very much alive, so why should I be seeing an aura which tells me you're not?"

I shook my head. "I don't know."

Dana jerked her head at Laurel, and her red curls shimmered in the firelight. "You told us she's a precog," she said, directing her words at Laurel.

"She is," Laurel said, eager in her response. "She knows something is going to happen in Sage Springs. I told her about the Disruptive Convergence, and about—"

"You did what?" Dana snapped, her green eyes flashing with anger.

"She knows something bad is going to happen in Sage Springs. She's already seen it, and she's seen the pools too. Flynn took her there."

"Flynn? Damn him. I should have known a pretty face would get in the way of his duty."

Okay, I'd had enough of them talking about me like I wasn't there. But I had no intention of telling them Riley had also taken me to the pools, and that we'd dumped a dead body there. "Look, Dana, I understand your concern, but I'm no threat to you, or anyone else. I want to help. I want to understand exactly what is going on here and do something to stop it."

She shook her head. "I don't know if it can be stopped."

My eyes widened. "It has to be! If we don't, it could mean the end of every one who lives in Sage Springs. I'm not sure, but it might spread even further. Everyone is in danger here, we have to do something."

"We can't change the pattern of the planets," she said.

I shook my head. "It isn't just because of the planets. Someone here, in Sage Springs, causes what's going to happen."

She gave a cold laugh. "How can you say that? Nothing is more powerful than the Convergence."

"Maybe not, but someone is going to use that power, and it creates what I've seen. Please believe me."

"Why should we?"

I tried to think of something I knew that would help her believe I was on her side.

"The carnival guys definitely have something to do with it," I said. "They made the accident happen on purpose so they could stay in town while the Disruptive Convergence was happening. They knew the cops would shut them down while they investigated the accident. Of course, they hadn't expected for me to see it before it happened. They'd been expecting people to be more badly hurt than they were."

Dana's eyes narrowed again. "How do you know this?"

I had to lie, at least a little. "I picked it up off one of the carny guys when he pushed me to get me off the midway."

"What were you doing at the carnival?"

I shrugged. "Snooping around. I knew something was up with that place, I wanted to know what."

"And what did you find out?"

"Nothing more than I've already told you." I thought for a moment. "But I might know someone who I can ask." I wasn't sure how Riley would react to me asking him about this stuff. Our relationship was still so new, fragile, careful pieces slotted together. I didn't want to do anything to jeopardize that, but if I didn't, there might not be an 'us' to save.

"Who?" said Dana.

"I don't want to tell you. Sorry."

"I thought you were on our side," said Laurel.

"I am. But the carny guys are really private. If he knows I'm trying to get information out of him, he might just shut down on me."

Kayla gave a smirk. "I know who she's talking about. It's that hot guy on the motorbike you've been hanging around with."

Laurel turned to me. "The same one working the ride that night?"

Suspicion thickened the air like syrup. "How do we know she's not here to get information for them?" Melissa declared.

I sighed and rolled my eyes. "Because I'm not. What possible information do you have that they would want?"

"There's a spell we can do," Dana said. "An honesty spell. It will show us the truth about you."

I blanched. I didn't want them to conduct any spells to do with me. There was a good chance they would not only find out that I was half vampire—from past experience I was aware vampires and witches had a long standing hatred of each other—but also that I was responsible for the murder of Jordy, a death I felt sure would become public knowledge in the next day or two. As long as the Convergence didn't end everyone and everything in Sage Springs, that was.

They took my hesitation as an admission of guilt.

Melissa lifted her hand and pointed a finger at me. "See! I knew she couldn't be trusted."

I wanted to cry in frustration. "You're wrong! I only want to help. Something is coming tomorrow night, and I've seen what it will do to everyone. It'll take their souls, everyone in this town!"

They exchanged worried glances.

"I won't let you do spells on me. It might affect my ability to predict things, or see things about people, and I can't afford for that to happen."

"The spell is safe," said Dana.

"So you say, but how do I know I can trust you? It goes both ways, you know, and I've hardly been welcomed in with open arms. I thought you liked me, Dana. I thought you saw something in my writing, but all along you were spying on me."

"I always liked your writing, Beth. The offer to join my staff had nothing to do with what's happening now. As for spying on you, well, I had to do what I had to do."

Anger roiled within me. "By sending your little spies after me? And what about Flynn? I assume he's in on this, too?"

"Flynn is the guardian of the pools. Of course he knows."

I thought back to how a wind seemed to have frightened him away from the very place he was supposed to be guarding. "For a guardian, he's not doing a very good job."

"This is harder for Flynn. He feels the water so much more intensely. The position of the planets has already created a change in the depth of the pools, the divide between the two worlds has grown thin, the water more shallow, even if it looks the same as it always has. He can tell a change is coming, and it's unnerved him. He's not himself."

"If he can control the water, can't he just make it deeper again?"

"He's tried, but something is working against him. Another force."

"From below?"

"We don't think so. Until the Convergence, the other world's magic can't affect us. We think it's someone else with great power."

"Maybe someone from the carnival?" I suggested.

Dana nodded, seeming to appreciate the suggestion. "Yes, perhaps. It would explain why they've stayed in town."

"But what would they achieve by doing this?"

"Maybe power. Perhaps they have a way of harnessing the darkness for themselves."

Something occurred to me. "Did Flynn take me to the pools for a reason? Did he want to check if they had a reaction to me?"

"I don't know. Did he?"

I thought of the reaction the pools had. They definitely responded, though I didn't think it was to me, and as far as I was aware, neither did Flynn. Besides, when I'd gone later with Riley, even considering what we'd been there to do, they'd not reacted in the same way. Something else had been responsible.

I couldn't worry about that now.

"Let me go back to the carnival, see what I can find out."

"One of us should go with you."

So you can keep an eye on me, I thought. "No, it's too dangerous. It's easier for me to go unseen, and my friend won't talk to me unless I'm alone."

Dana exchanged a glance with Laurel.

"I trust her," Laurel said, giving an apologetic shrug.

I could have hugged her.

"Okay, fine. Go alone," said Dana. "Meet us back here in two hours. The Convergence is almost upon us, and time is running out."

CHAPTER 20

I FOUND RILEY riding his bike inside the huge metal cage I'd seen him in the first night I'd come to the carnival. I stood back and watched him for a while, appreciating the air of danger combined with skill that his performance displayed.

I'd sneaked in the back route Riley had shown me, avoiding the midway and the people milling around. Riley had told me the carny folk were night owls, but there seemed to be more activity tonight than I'd seen since the place had been shut down. The air was filled with the clang of metal on metal, of the roar of machinery being used, of men shouting instructions to one another. I didn't like it. They were up to something.

Riley rode one final, dizzying loop and brought the bike to a skidding halt at the bottom of the cage. He must have sensed me standing there, hiding beside one of the trailers, for he turned and looked directly at me. I lifted a hand to wave, but he didn't respond, not even with a smile.

My heart sank. *What now?*

He opened the door in the cage and climbed out, dragging his bike with him. He left his bike beside the cage and ran over to me with a slow, easy lollop. "Icy, what are you doing here?"

"I need to talk to you."

"Yeah, I need to talk to you, too." He grabbed my hand. "Come with me."

"Where are we going?"

"To my trailer. There's a lot of people around tonight. It's too easy for you to be seen."

I looked again toward the midway, where people worked on the rides, unscrewing bolts and taking things apart. "What's going on, Riley?"

"Just come with me."

He led me to his trailer, drawing me inside its now familiar warmth and atmosphere. But instead of pulling me into his arms, as I had hoped, he stood in front of me, his arms folded across his chest, his lips pressed together, a line between his deep blue eyes.

"What is it, Riley? You're scaring me."

"We got the okay from the police department that no foul play was involved in the accident on the Waltzer. We're allowed to move on."

The ground shifted under my feet, dropping away, together with my stomach, leaving me weak and empty. My head spun. "You're leaving?"

"We missed the slot for our next pitch a couple of towns along, so we don't have anywhere to go until tomorrow night, but yeah, we're leaving."

"You're leaving?" I repeated, unable to make the words feel true. My voice sounded tiny, disbelieving, even to my own ears. "No, you can't leave me. Not now."

"I'm sorry, Icy. You must have realized I'd move on at some point. The carnival is my home. These are my people."

No, I wanted to cry. *I'm your people now.*

But I couldn't get the words to come out.

"How could you?" I said instead. "How could you be with me, knowing you were going to leave?" My heart was surely breaking, fracturing into tiny pieces. I felt it would shatter through me, slicing me into so many parts no one would ever be able to put me back together again. How stupid I had been. Of course he was always going to leave me.

"Baby, please ..." He reached out to me.

I slapped his hand away. "Don't 'baby' me."

"I'll stay in touch. I'll call you. I'll come back and visit when I can."

I shook my head, staring at his face and wondering how something so beautiful could cause so much pain. Tears built inside me, swelling like a balloon inside my chest, rising to create a painful lump in my throat and making the backs of my eyes burn. "It won't be the same."

He stepped toward me, moving into my personal space, his arms slipping around my waist. He pulled me to him, and I couldn't resist. Though I was furious at him, I was also hurt, and he was the only one who could make the hurt go away. I pressed my face against his chest, the familiar sensation of leather against my skin. I inhaled the scent of him, the warmth of his body heating my cheek, trying to commit the moment to memory. I didn't know how many more times I'd be able to do this.

Riley pressed his nose and mouth against the top of my head, kissing my hair. "I don't want to leave you." His breath heated my scalp.

I moved away from him slightly so I could look into his face. "So don't. Stay here, with me."

He gave a laugh, but it didn't contain any humor. "What, in your dorm room? That's hardly going to go down well."

"I could hide you under the bed."

He quickly kissed me on the lips. "Tempting," he said with a sad smile.

I knew I was being ridiculous. He was right. It wasn't as if I had my own place. He lived in a trailer. He was a daredevil motorbike rider in a carnival. Who was I to try and tie him to one place, to make him give up his adventurous life and get a regular job down at the local store?

I was torturing myself being here with him. If he really cared for me, wouldn't he figure out some way to stay?

You could always go with him, a little voice suggested in my head.

No, I couldn't. My parents would freak if I told them I'd run off with a traveling carnival. And yet that little voice persisted. *You expect him to change his life for you, but you're not willing to do the same.*

"I really care about you, Icy," he said, brushing my cheek with the back of his thumb.

"You care about me?" I spat. For some reason the words tasted bitter in my mouth. *Care* about me? Had I wanted more? Did I feel more for him? Had I hoped for the word 'love' to come from his lips?

"Of course I do." He seemed surprised, completely unaware of the reason for my anger.

"Well, that just makes everything okay again, doesn't it? So good to know that by sleeping with me, it means you care about me. You care so much, you can just take off and leave me here alone."

I couldn't stop the tears now. They spilled from my eyes, wetting my cheeks. My nose grew stuffy. I probably looked like a snotty child throwing a temper tantrum, but I didn't care. He'd done this. He'd hurt me. I wanted him to experience my pain.

"Icy, I didn't plan this! It's my life!"

I pushed past him to get out of the trailer. I had to get out of there. "Well, enjoy living it, especially now you won't have the complication of having me around."

Shoving open the door, I burst out into the warm night and stumbled down the steps to get away. I'd never experienced this kind of pain before. I wanted him to chase after me and tell me that he didn't mean it, that he would stay here for me, but the rational part of my mind knew that wouldn't happen. I couldn't ask him, or expect him to give up his whole life because of a girl he'd known for less than a week. Even though I knew that, it didn't stop the pain. How could I get through each day knowing I wouldn't feel the touch of his skin on mine, taste his mouth, just be with him?

I ran away from the carnival, heading across the fields, toward the forest and the darkness of the trees. Tears streamed down my face, I could barely see for crying.

Suddenly, I realized I'd completely forgotten the reason I'd gone to see Riley in the first place. Here was I worrying about not being with him, when our worlds could be about to alter forever tonight anyway.

I wasn't far from the trees now.

Was that his voice calling to me? I wanted him to come after me more than anything. I turned my head, to see if I could spot him, slowing my run. Riley wasn't there. His voice had been in my head.

As I turned back around, I slammed into a massive body. Arms wrapped around me, but they weren't gentle or affectionate.

I opened my mouth to scream, but as soon as I did, a strong hand grabbed my face and shoved something into my mouth—earthy and gritty. The effect was immediate. The inside of my mouth began to burn. The fingers tightened on my cheeks, squeezing against my teeth, and forcing my lips to open. Water was poured down my throat, forcing me to either choke or swallow.

I swallowed.

The strong arms let me go.

I screamed and staggered away, falling to the ground. I scrabbled backward, gagging and spitting. My insides felt like they were on fire, as if flames licked and crept up through my stomach, spreading into my heart, for my blood to transfer the fire to my veins. All the strength I had burned away in the flames, leaving me weak and helpless. Through my pain, I got the briefest of moments to take in the people who now stood, towering over me.

The man was built like a body-builder, with an almost non-existent neck, massive shoulders, and a bald head. He had a pug nose and small eyes from which he stared down at me. I caught a glimpse of tattoos on his knuckles.

I knew this man. It was Bulldog Mackenzie, the guy I'd only caught a glimpse of from a distance before, the guy people referred to as 'The Bull.' I could see why.

Two other men stood either side of The Bull. I recognized them as Russ and Mitch, the two men who'd been with Jordy the night I'd killed him for almost raping me.

"See," said Russ, the smaller of the two. "I knew what she was!"

"A vampire, huh?" The Bull mused. "A real life vampire."

I wanted to correct him, but what the hell was the point?

"Told you the aconite root would work," Russ continued, clearly pleased with himself. "I looked it up on the internet."

"Yes, very interesting. Who would have thought a simple herb could have such an effect? Now that she's weak, I suggest we kill her."

From his belt, The Bull produced a huge knife, the glint of the blade catching in the moonlight. He bent to me and hauled me up backward, the knife placed against my throat. I wanted to writhe in pain, but I daren't move because of the proximity of the blade to my jugular.

"No!"

The shout came from a distance away, but all three men looked toward it. Through the haze of agony that held me in its grip, I caught sight of Riley running toward us.

"No! Wait!" he yelled. "You don't want to kill her."

"And why's that, Riley?" Bull said. "Because you've gotten yourself a crush on the little lady?" He snorted. "If you can call her a lady."

Riley's eyes flicked to me. I could see the agony within their deep depths. He was going to save me, surely. I didn't know how, but I was sure Riley wouldn't want me dead.

"If she's what you say she is—" he started, only to be interrupted by a shout from the other guy, Mitch.

"She is! She bit out Jordy's throat. Right in front of us!"

Riley gave him a cold glare, and continued. "If she's what you say she is, you should use her tonight. Screw the other girl. This one will give you more."

The Bull's grip relaxed just a fraction of an inch. "I thought the other one was who we needed to sacrifice. You've been working all that magic on her. You said we needed her because her parents own the land the pools are on, that it makes her tied to the land, that her death will have special consequences."

Riley wouldn't look at me, but my heart pounded so hard I thought it might explode. Riley had been the one conducting the magic on Brooke? Please don't let it be true.

"It's true," he said, as if answering my silent plea, and a part of my soul cried out. "Brooke's death during the

Disruptive Convergence will give you great power. But *her* death will give you more."

The Bull's eyes gleamed with greedy hunger. "More? What could be more?"

"Because of what she is, if you take her life in the pool during the Convergence, the other side will give you immortality."

CHAPTER 21

A MOAN OF pain escaped my lips—pain from the herbs they'd forced me to swallow, and pain from learning Riley wanted me dead.

"I'll take her back to my trailer until tonight," said Riley. "I can keep an eye on her there."

But Bulldog laughed. "I don't think so."

Riley frowned. "After everything I've done, don't you trust me?"

"Oh sure, I trust you, but I don't trust that thing in your pants. I know what it's like to be your age, when everything revolves around whether you're going to get lucky or not."

"I'm not like that." Riley scowled.

He snorted. "'Course you're not. She's coming back with me."

Bulldog released his hold around my neck, lowering the knife so he held it loosely at my waist. If I was at my normal strength, I could easily have grabbed the wrist holding the knife, and twisted the weapon from his grip, probably snapping a bone or two at the same time. But I wasn't up to my normal strength. I'd never felt so weak in my life.

With his free hand, he grabbed both of my slender wrists. His big hand easily circled both wrists, crushing the bones together. Though painful, it was nothing compared to the fire still raging within me. I felt as though every internal organ was burning, and soon smoke would start pouring from every orifice, until I crumbled into a small pile of ash and blew away in the wind.

Bulldog started to drag me back toward the carnival and the group of trailers gathered at the rear. The deconstruction of the midway was still underway, most of the carnies completely unaware of what was happening in the fields behind them. The sounds of metal clanging, engines thrumming, men shouting instruction to one another filled the night air.

Riley chased after us. "If you want this to work, I'll have to conduct some of the same rituals on her instead of Brooke."

"I still want the other girl," Bulldog replied.

"But you don't need her. This one will give you so much more."

"So you say, but if it doesn't work, I want backup. Besides, we've already done so much work on the blonde, no point in wasting it. I've been looking forward to seeing her peachy skin bleed."

We stopped outside of a large trailer. This one was brand new and at least four times the size of Riley's home. Bulldog entered first, dragging me up the steps behind him. My feet caught on the metal slats, my ankles banging painfully against them.

The interior was gaudily decorated, with the couch in black leather, and a glass and chrome table. A lion-skin rug spread out on the floor, the lion's mouth open in a permanent growl, its black eyes glassy. I imagined Bulldog's bedcovers would be something animal print, probably with black sheets below. I shook the thought from my head. I really didn't want to be thinking anything about The Bull's bed right now.

He slung me down to the floor. I landed with my face only inches away from the lion's. I felt sorry for him. Here we were, both predators, both reduced to lying on some scumbag's floor.

But at least I was still alive.

Bulldog turned to Mitch and Russ. "Go and get the other girl. We won't have long until the planets are aligned. We need to be ready."

Mitch nodded and disappeared out the way we'd come in.

I groaned and started to push myself to sitting. Riley dropped down at my side, his hand on my arm as though to help me up, but I shook him off. "Don't touch me!"

"Icy," he said, almost begging. His eyes flicked to where Bulldog stared down at us both. He dropped my arm and moved away.

"Don't you have preparations to make?" The Bull said, his eyes like stone as he stared in Riley's direction.

Riley ducked his head. "Sure, Bulldog. I'm on it."

He disappeared into another part of the trailer, only giving me a fleeting glance as he did so.

The Bull stood over me, a hulking mountain with me in its shadow. For a moment, I thought he was going to kick me. I wished vehemently for my strength to return, but the twigs or roots, or whatever they'd force fed me still burned in my stomach, and I barely thought myself capable of lifting my own head off the floor. As soon as the stuff wore off, I swore Bulldog Mackenzie would meet the same end as Jordy. My anger was like a red cloud, encompassing my entire being, and I gritted my teeth. I would make him pay for this. He would see who he was dealing with, and I'd make him regret it.

"I can't believe a tiny little thing like you could take out someone like Jordy." I could hear laughter in his voice, as if this whole thing was no more than another game, a real life ride in his carnival.

"Size isn't everything," I managed to spit.

"Clearly Jordy didn't know that, huh?" The look he gave me made me think he even had a tiny bit of appreciation for the murder I'd committed. Not that he'd appreciated one of his own being killed, more that he admired anyone capable of taking a life.

I coughed, the herbs in my gut burning up my throat like acid. "Jordy was asking for it."

My attention was drawn beyond Bulldog as Riley came back into the main part of the trailer. He held a number of items in his hands, but I struggled to make out what they were from the floor—a bowl, and a number of candles, along with a few other items.

My traitorous heart still swelled at the sight of him.

I didn't want to hate him; I cared about him too much to bring myself to hate him. But right now, I wanted to grab him by the shoulders and shake him so hard his brain rattled in his head, and yell in his face to ask him what the hell he was doing.

He set his items down on a table, and positioned himself with his back to me, blocking my view. Damn him if he couldn't even look at me!

A knock came at the door.

The Bull turned at the sound. "What?" he barked.

The door cracked open and a tall, skinny woman, a slash of red lipstick across her mouth, most of which had bled into the lines around her lips, stepped into the space. "Hey, Bull. Hunter needs you over at his commission."

Bulldog's eyes narrowed. "Can't he deal with it? I'm kinda busy here."

"No, sorry, he can't. It's an emergency." The woman's eyes flicked to me, and I wondered if she knew exactly why I was there. "We don't want another accident happening."

Bulldog sighed. "Fine. Russ, you're in charge here. No one leaves my trailer, and no one except Mitch and the other girl gets in. Got it?"

He nodded. "Got it, Bull."

Bulldog pointed at Riley. "And you behave yourself. I've got eyes on you."

"Jesus, Bull. What have I ever done against you?"

The Bull's eyes flicked briefly to me. Riley might have betrayed me, but The Bull was sharp enough to have picked up on the fact there was something between me and Riley. Or at least there had been.

"You've got preparations to get on with, haven't you?" he said to Riley.

Riley pressed his lips together and nodded, still not looking at me.

"Don't worry, Boss," said Russ. "I've got backup." He tapped his hip, just below his jacket. I noticed Riley tense. Was the other guy implying he was armed? It wouldn't surprise me if he was.

Bulldog threw me a frown, clearly not wanting to leave me alone, and then slammed from the trailer. The atmosphere changed as soon as he was gone, and not in a good way. The guard on me had effectively fallen to one person, and I could tell he took his role seriously. I didn't want to contemplate the idea that he had an itchy trigger finger.

Russ took up position on the couch, his arms resting on his knees. He leaned forward, brows drawn together as he stared at me. I scowled back.

I wanted to get a glimpse at what Riley was doing. I needed to shift my position slightly, so I was side on to Riley, instead of lying with him with his back to me.

Wanting an excuse to move, I started to fake a coughing fit, which quickly turned into a real one due to the acid burning up my throat and being breathed back in again, hitting my lungs. Though weak, I rolled across the lion skin rug, to come to rest with my back against an arm chair which matched the huge, black leather couch.

Russ reached out and nudged me with his foot, hard enough to hurt. "Where the hell do you think you're going?" I couldn't answer, just continued to cough, my lungs burning, tears streaming from my eyes, clear snot from my nose.

"Jesus, Russ," Riley exclaimed, glancing over to me, his eyes wide with concern. "Leave her alone."

"You never saw what the little bitch did to Jordy," Russ snapped. "She needs to pay." His hand moved to his hip, and Riley froze, one hand out held.

I managed to get a hold on my cough and propped my back against the chair, trying to shrink myself into the leather and vanish.

"Hey, it's all right, Russ," Riley said in a calm tone. "She's going to get what's coming, don't you worry. But you know The Bull's got plans for her. You wouldn't want to go messing those up now, would you?"

At the mention of Bulldog, Russ's hand dropped from his hip. "Fine," he spat. "Though Bull would have killed her out on the field if you hadn't interfered."

"Yeah, well I'm just trying to do what's best for all of us." His gaze flicked over to me, and I tried to read what was in its blue depth. "Anyway," he continued. "I've got work to do now, so I need some quiet to concentrate. Got it?"

Russ gave a sniff of disdain. "Fine. I've gotta take a piss anyway."

He turned his back and headed deeper into the trailer, to find, I assumed, the bathroom.

Riley turned back to the table and collected his things together, and then approached me. I watched him with wariness, unsure of what was going to happen next. He held five small pillar candles, which he placed around me, not seeming to care that the chair I leaned against was also surrounded.

"They're for the points of the elements," he told me, as he got to work lighting them with a lighter he removed from his pocket. As he set fire to each wick, he spoke their name. "Earth, Fire, Water, Spirit, and finally, my element, Air." As he lit the fifth candle, the wick burst into flame higher than any of the others, scorching into the air.

"What the hell are you?" I said. "Some kind of witch?" I sought my mind for the male equivalent. "Or a warlock?"

He shook his head. "I'm an Elemental. I have powers, but my main power is that I can control the air."

I opened my mouth to say, 'Like Flynn,' but promptly shut it again. There was a chance Riley didn't know about Flynn, and that could be used to my advantage.

I thought back to all of the weather anomalies I'd experienced since getting to Sage Springs. From first entering the town when the wind had suddenly dropped, allowing my escape from my car, to the way a gust must have burst the window open in my bedroom. I'd seen him that first day, I realized. He'd been standing in the field, watching the events of the fallen power line. I'd even caught the scent of him—leather and motorcycle oil—on the air. Had he controlled the air enough to allow me to run from the car?

"It's how I always knew when you were in trouble. A small part of me, you could call it my soul, I guess, is able to travel on the wind, to see and sense things happening somewhere else when my body is right here. Ever since I first laid eyes on you, a part of me has been following you."

"Following me? Do you know how creepy that sounds?"

I guessed in the big scheme of things, it didn't matter, but I hated the thought of being watched.

He shrugged. "I was worried you'd get yourself into trouble, and I wasn't too far wrong."

"Seems to me all my trouble started around you."

He didn't respond. Instead, he pulled out a small, clear bag of white powder.

"Are you going to drug me now?" I challenged.

He gave a sad smile and tipped the powder into a bowl. "No, this is white ash. Its use is powerful in communing with the other side, and other worlds." He bent his head over the bowl and muttered a few words I didn't understand. Then he held his hand above it and circled his index finger clockwise and then counter-clockwise. As he did so, the powder began to move, just the slightest vibration at first, and then more, until finally the ash rose into the air in a spiral. I was mesmerized, the spectacle almost beautiful, especially with Riley being the one in control.

But then he snapped his fingers together, and moved his hand away, and the ash dropped back into the bowl. Riley lowered his head again, and spat into the ash, and stirred it around with his finger, creating a paste.

He dipped his finger into the paste and brought it to my skin. I flinched.

"I'm not going to hurt you."

"Really? That's not what Bulldog thinks."

He began to trace lines over my skin. I hated to admit it, but his touch still sent a trickle of desire running through me. Goosebumps appeared where his finger dragged across my flesh. He started at my hand, creating swirls, dips, lines and circles. As if writing. He moved from my hands, up to my arms. As soon as the white paste was applied to my skin, it vanished. I realized he was drawing the runes I'd seen on Brooke.

Movement came from the doorway leading to the back of the trailer and I realized Russ had entered the room again.

"You need to trust me, Icy." Riley said, his voice low.

"How am I supposed to do that?" I hissed. The pain from the herbs they'd force fed me remained. I wished I had my strength so I could rip the lot of them to pieces. "You practically handed me to them on a platter!"

Russ called out, "Hey, Riley. No chatting with the sacrifice."

"I'm not chatting," he snapped back. "I have to be able to speak for the magic to work."

I heard Russ mutter, "Damn mumbo-jumbo," under his breath, but then he turned away and started to fiddle with the cuffs on his shirt.

I glared at Riley. "I know you people caused the accident on the Waltzer on purpose," I said, my voice barely above a whisper.

He squinted at me. "Yeah, so?"

"Jesus, Riley! People could have been killed!"

"Collateral damage," he growled.

"For what? I assume all this has to do with the Disruptive Convergence."

"How do you know about that?"

I didn't answer his question. "What about the hell cycle that follows?"

"We'll be protected."

"Why? Because you sacrifice people? I can't believe I ever trusted you!" Tears were close again, but I fought against them, not wanting him to see my weakness. "I didn't just trust you, Riley. I gave myself to you. Do you have any idea what that meant for me?"

His hand closed around my wrist, gripping it tight. "It meant something to me too, Icy. Don't ever think it didn't."

"What else am I supposed to think?"

"Hey, you weren't exactly honest with me either. You never told me about being a vamp."

"Part vampire," I corrected him with a sniff.

"Yeah, well, you kept that quiet, so don't make out like you're all sweetness and innocence. And you never admitted to me the part about being able to see the future."

I looked at him with tears swimming in my eyes, blurring my vision. "Guess I'm not so good at the predicting the future part," I said. "Or else I'd have seen you betray me."

CHAPTER 22

THE DOOR BURST open, making me jump.

Brooke came walking up the steps, her blonde hair loose around her face, the moonlight behind glowing through her locks like a halo. Mitch followed her close behind.

My roommate looked around the trailer with a dreamy smile on her face. No part of her acted as though she'd been kidnapped, or that something unimaginable was going to happen in a matter of hours.

"Brooke?" I said.

She blinked at me and smiled. "Hey, Beth. How are you doing?"

We could have been meeting at a social. No, that was wrong. If we'd been at a social, Brooke would have been glaring at me with her usual contempt and probably ignoring my existence. Instead, she smiled at me as though I was an old friend she'd just bumped into.

"Brooke, are you okay?"

"Sure, Beth. I'm great."

I turned to Riley. "What have you done to her?"

"Nothing you need to worry about. It's a simple contentment spell, that's all. She's probably happier now than she is normally."

I couldn't argue with that, but I still didn't like seeing Brooke like this. Even though no narcotics had been used, the way she was acting felt too close to her being drugged.

Something about how he'd managed to change her behavior made me uncomfortable and nauseous. Had he done this to me, too? Had I fallen for him because of some kind of spell? I didn't want to even think about what that meant in regards to me sleeping with him.

I shook my head in hurt and bewilderment at Riley. "I can't believe I got you so wrong."

But hadn't I seen darkness in him? Hadn't his air of danger drawn me to him in the first place? The darkness I'd recognized in him was the same as I knew was within me. I was a fool not to expect the situation to blow up in my face.

I was aware of both Mitch and Russ watching Riley and me. Riley opened his mouth to respond and then closed it again. Instead, he gave his head a slight shake and turned away from me, his lips pressed together. I blinked back my tears while Brooke watched on, a beatific smile on her perfect face.

The door slammed open, grabbing everyone's attention.

"God-damned idiots," The Bull growled, barging into the trailer, his size immediately taking up a large amount of space. "Sometimes I wonder if they'd be able to wipe their own asses if I wasn't around."

"Everything okay, Boss?" Russ asked, his hands clenching and unclenching anxiously.

"Fine, but the clock's ticking, and we need to get this show on the road." His eyes locked on Brooke, and his eyebrows lifted. "Good to see we've got everyone we need. Now haul ass. You know where you're going."

Mitch took Brooke by the arm and dragged her past Bulldog and back out into the open air. She didn't need to be dragged. I had a feeling she'd have gone anywhere she was told, but Mitch seemed to like to assert his strength over her.

Russ approached me and reached down to grab my arm.

I yanked away. "I don't need you to drag me around." I still felt impossibly weak, though the fire raging in my stomach seemed to have abated. Using the chair behind me, I pulled myself to my feet. The ground felt unstable beneath me, my legs wobbly. I teetered for a moment, and Riley reached out and grabbed me before I fell. I pulled away from him, too. "I don't want you anywhere near me."

"You can't walk, Icy. Would you rather I help you, or shall we let Russ do it?" I glanced over to Russ, who licked his lips as he sneered at me.

"Fine," I relented. Despite everything, I would rather have Riley's hands on me than Russ's.

I leaned against Riley, allowing his strength to hold me up as I took step after unsteady step out of the trailer. His arm was around my waist, his familiar scent and warmth encasing me. I wanted more than anything to give into the ache in my heart, to have him hold me and tell me this was all a big mistake, but I knew that wasn't going to happen. I forced myself to be strong, to build a wall around my heart against him, but nothing in my life had ever been harder.

Russ, Mitch, and Brooke waited for us outside. We stepped off the small set of metal steps and onto the dirt ground. Bulldog followed us out, locking the door of his trailer, before joining us.

My legs buckled again, and Riley grabbed me, holding me up.

"She's struggling to walk," he said to Bulldog. "Why don't I take her on my bike and meet you there?"

The Bull gave a snort of laughter. "Yeah, right. So you can whisk her away to lover's paradise, you mean?"

Riley snapped. "Would you quit that? You've been like a father to me, Bull. You looked after my mom before she died. You could have kicked me out of the carnival, but you didn't. You kept me on, and trained me, and kept me clothed and fed. I've done everything you've asked of me. Now you keep acting like I've betrayed you."

The Bull was smarter than I'd given him credit for. He gave Riley a cold, intense stare. "Never trust someone completely, son. The moment you do, that's when they'll get you," he pounded his chest, "right here. Straight through the heart." He pointed a finger at Riley. "Even the most faithful dog has the capacity to turn around and bite you in the ass. Don't you ever forget it."

"Yes, sir," Riley said, but I didn't miss the tightness in his jaw.

We were all outside now, standing beside the trailer. Looking toward the midway, I noticed several of the rides had been dismantled, the huge structures remaining now appearing awkward and out of place. Though it must be approaching midnight, the carnies still worked, their voices carrying over to us in the night air. I considered screaming for help, but I doubted anyone would hear me above the clanging of machinery, music, and shouting men. Even if they did hear me, who would help? The Bull ran the show, and they wouldn't challenge his authority—not if they still wanted a commission at the next town.

Bulldog lifted his face to the sky, and, in a moment of unusual serenity, smiled up at the stars. "Well, look at that," he said. "It's already happening."

I looked up to the night sky and gasped. The moon was full, appearing huge and yellow. It was close enough to allow me to see all the shadows and craters that made up its surface. It was beautiful. But that wasn't all. Several of the stars appeared far larger and brighter than I'd ever seen them, their radiance, together with the moon, making the night far less dark than usual. Though light still spilled from Bulldog's trailer, I knew as we headed across the fields and into the forest, that we wouldn't need flashlights to help us find our way.

The hairs on my arms began to stand to attention, the hair on my head beginning to lift as though someone had placed a balloon covered in static electricity close me. I lifted my hand to touch my head, checking my hair wasn't literally standing on end.

Riley spotted me doing so. "It's the proximity of the moon," he told me. It's affecting our electrical fields. You might find yourself breathless too, the closer the moon gets, so try not to panic."

I didn't think a bit of breathlessness was going to be my main concern.

He pointed at the sky. "See the one farthest to the right, the brightest one?" I nodded. "That's Procyon." He moved his arm to point farther left. "And see the one that's the least bright? That's called Capella. And the one in the middle is Rigel." I felt his breath on the back of my ear, the heat of his body against my back. "In another hour, all of those stars will be aligned with the moon, and that's when we'll experience the Disruptive Convergence."

My heart ran cold. "And when you'll kill everyone in Sage Springs."

"I'm not killing anyone, Icy."

"But you'll play your part."

He didn't answer.

The Bull started forward. "Enough standing around," he said. "Let's get moving."

We headed away from the trailers, toward the fields behind the carnival where they'd first captured me, and to the forests beyond.

I felt as though I was willingly walking toward my death. I was tempted to simply not bother to move my feet, and force them to carry me, but I didn't want Bulldog, Russ, or Mitch's hands on me. Besides, what would it achieve? No one around here was going to help me. Also, as much as I didn't want these particular people for company, I had to at least be at the pools during the Disruptive Convergence. I had no idea what I could do to stop it, but if I wasn't there, Sage Springs wouldn't stand a chance.

I hated that I needed to use Riley's strength to keep me upright, but as we left the trailers behind and headed into the depths of the trees, a tingling began in my legs and arms, a burning in my muscles that had nothing to do with the herbs they'd fed me, and everything to do with my strength returning. I made no more effort than previously to walk, not wanting to alert them to the fact the herbs were wearing off. The last thing I wanted was to suffer another dose. If that happened, I would stand no chance of surviving the next hour. At least this time I would be prepared for them. If they came anywhere near me with that stuff, I would bite their fingers off before they had a chance to get it in my mouth.

As we walked through the trees, following a small trail, I realized the forest felt different tonight. At first, I struggled to pinpoint exactly what the change was, but then it dawned on me. Other than the sounds of our feet crunching against twigs and leaves, and the heavy breathing of the unfit men ahead, the forest was utterly silent. No insects buzzed or whined near my head, no animals scurried away from us in the undergrowth. Even the birds roosting overhead were gone. It was like the strange emptiness of the pools had spread its boundaries, causing all life in the forest to scatter to safety.

All life except us.

CHAPTER 23

THE WALK THROUGH the forest was starting to sap my strength again. Though the light from the moon and stars was bright, brighter than it would probably ever be again, the darkness caused by the trees made the route harder than in the daytime. I found myself tripping over hidden roots and fallen branches. On those occasions, I was thankful for Riley holding me up.

I stumbled again and turned my ankle over. Pain shot up through my ankle and calf, and I hissed air in between my teeth.

Riley stopped with me. "Are you okay?" he asked, looking down at me with concern.

"Fine," I snapped, not liking him seeing me at my weakest. I ignored the pain and kept walking, using Riley as my crutch.

But the effect of the herb was wearing off, the weakness that had held me in its clutches abating with every minute that passed. I just hoped it would be gone from my system by the time Bulldog decided to kill me.

As Riley had warned me, the air grew thin, and I fought to take a deep breath. I noticed the men in front struggled worse, their large forms needing more oxygen to replenish their muscles while they were on the move.

Good, I thought bitterly. I hoped they felt like they were drowning.

Brooke barely seemed to notice anything was wrong, and strode on, as though out for a Sunday hike.

We were getting closer to the pools now; I sensed their presence in the atmosphere. But that wasn't the only thing getting closer. Every so often I caught a glimpse of the moon and stars between the tree branches. The moon was huge and had taken on a red glow. It was both magnificent, and terrifying.

"There's blood on the moon," I muttered beneath my breath. The hairs on my arms now stood at full attention, as though I was freezing cold instead of warm and traipsing through a forest on a balmy night. I imagined my normally frizz-heaven hair would be twice its regular size by now.

"Maybe it's a sign," Riley said.

I glanced up at him. His expression was unreadable as he stared ahead, just keeping his feet moving, his arm still around my waist. Whatever the sign meant, I didn't think it would be a good one.

My lungs were starting to burn now, and a flutter of panic tickled my heart. What if the air grew so thin I was unable to breathe? Would we all die before we even reached the pools? Perhaps that would be a good thing, and the Disruptive Convergence would pass without further event?

"Here," Riley said, noticing my breathing. "I can help."

His eyes closed briefly and he spoke in almost silent whispers. A sudden breeze lifted around us, stirring my hair. He reached out, as though catching something in the space in front of us, and he brought his cupped hand to my mouth and nose.

"Breathe," he told me.

I didn't have much choice. My lungs were already burning from the thin air, and I hadn't yet caught my breath. I inhaled, expecting the shallow breath I'd managed before, but instead my lungs filled with oxygen rich air.

Instantly, my chest expanded, letting go of the tight wheeziness I'd been suffering with most of the hike. My head cleared, the building panic abated. I doubted the relief would last, but for the moment I was grateful.

"How did you do that?" I asked, staring up at him, curiously.

He gave me a wink. "A magician never shares his secrets."

I scowled. "I hope you're not flirting with me, Riley Draiodh. Especially considering the situation!"

He shook his head and kept walking. "I wouldn't dream of it."

I started to recognize the path we were on, the fallen tree trunk which Riley had needed to skirt around when we'd come here on his bike. The boulder completely covered in moss on one side. The low lying swathe of branches which were low enough to brush my hair and force the men to duck beneath. My heart picked up its pace, thumping against the inside of my chest. What would we find when we got there? What would happen to Brooke and me? The words 'bleeding' and 'sacrifice' had been mentioned, so I was certain it wouldn't be good.

Out of nowhere, Riley pulled up short, forcing me to stop with him. "Wait!"

Bulldog turned at the sound of his voice, and the others stopped too. "What now?" Bull demanded. "We need to move. We've only got another thirty minutes, at most."

"We're not alone," Riley called out. "Some people have already made it to the pools."

My heart leaped. Of course, Laurel, Dana, and the others. Would they have realized something was wrong when I'd not come back to the beach? Had they come here to find me, perhaps finally taking me at my word that the Disruptive Convergence was going to be far more treacherous than they knew? But then my heart sank again. This put them in danger. How far would The Bull go to get what he wanted? He wasn't afraid of committing a little murder among friends, but would he really kill four college girls? I understood him wanting me dead, I was hardly a normal girl, but they were innocent.

He's willing to kill Brooke, I reminded myself. *She's done nothing to him.*

Had I only lured Laurel's circle to their deaths, or would they be able to do something to save us?

We followed Bulldog off the path and into the clearing.

My prediction about who was already here had been correct.

The girls sat on a patch of grass in the middle of the pools. Candles shone around them, and they held hands, chanting quietly. They barely seemed to register our arrival. I wanted to cry. They might not have come for me, they might have only come because of the pools and the Convergence, but they were here and that's what mattered.

"Kayla, hi!" Brooke squealed with excitement and waved frantically. Kayla's total lack of response did nothing to perturb her.

Bulldog started forward and suddenly rebounded back. "What the hell?"

For the first time, Riley left my side. I felt the space he'd left like an empty chasm beside me. I didn't want to feel that way, he was my enemy now, but I couldn't help myself.

He reached out into the space Bulldog had bounced back from. Laid his palm flat, as though pressing against a pane of glass. "They must be creating some kind of protective spell to keep us out."

Bulldog's eyes narrowed. "Can you fix it?"

Riley gave a curt nod. "Of course."

He placed both hands against the invisible surface and lowered his head as though in prayer. I stood watching, part in fear, part in fascination. Riley began to speak, though I was unable to pick up on the words, his voice was too low. My eyes darted between him and the group of girls sitting on a patch of grass between the pools.

As I watched, the leaves in the trees overhead began to rustle, and those on the ground gently lifted and flipped and swirled across the forest floor. The ferns began to bend, and the water stirred in ripples. Dana's long hair blew back from her face, and all of their clothing billowed.

Bizarrely, standing on the outskirts, I barely felt a breeze. I checked out Brooke and noted that her hair wasn't moving either. The wind was directed purely at the circle.

The force of the gusts grew stronger, causing the water to lift in waves, splashing on the surrounding ground. *I've seen this before,* I realized. The night Flynn brought me here. Had that been Riley then, too, sending us a warning? Or had it only been Flynn he'd been chasing off?

The wind had become a low moan, quickly rising to a howl. The candles flickered and spurted, before extinguishing completely.

The circle of witches clung tightly to one another's hands. Their hair whipped from their faces, Dana's red curls threatening to strangle her. Their clothing blew back from their bodies. The noise was tremendous, a shriek I'd only ever heard during a storm. The girls' chanting grew louder, trying to be heard over the wind, until their voices became a chorus of shouts.

"Hang in there," I willed them under my voice.

But they were starting to lose it. I caught Melissa shooting Dana a look of sheer panic, her skin pale. I hoped she wasn't about to have another fit.

I glanced up at the sky. The moon was blood red, the stars beginning to slip in line.

"Riley, quit it!" I yelled. "Leave them alone."

Bulldog glanced back at me and then turned to Russ. "Get her to shut the hell up."

Russ stalked toward me and lifted his hand. I saw it coming, but didn't get the chance to move. I still wasn't up to my normal strength. His hand came down in an arc, the palm catching my cheek and jaw, knocking me sideways. Pain exploded up one side of my face. I struggled to keep my balance, staggered to one side, and dropped to my knees.

"Hey!" Riley yelled, glaring with fury at Russ.

A cluster of pinecones flew toward Laurel. Instinctively, she lifted her hand to protect her face, and broke the circle. The girls fell silent, looking around themselves in confusion, unsure what to do next.

Riley dropped his hands, and the wind immediately fell away. He ran back to me and skidded to a halt beside me. He reached down to pick me up.

"Leave me alone."

He must have picked up that I wasn't kidding and turned his attention to Russ, instead. "Don't you ever lay a hand on her again!"

"Shut it, Riley," snapped Bulldog. "Have you forgotten whose side you're on?"

It didn't matter. The protective spell had been broken.

Bulldog pointed toward the circle. "Get the girls."

Mitch and Russ didn't need to be told twice. They stormed past the pools, toward the circle of witches.

Dana saw them coming and tried to regroup her circle. "Link hands. We have time to do something—"

But she was stopped in her tracks.

Melissa's eyes rolled, flashing the whites, and she fell backward, landing on the ground with a crack that made me wince. Her body jerked and juddered as she fitted in the dirt.

"What's happening to her?" I called out to the circle.

"It's the alignment of the stars," Laurel cried. "Her fits have been getting worse ever since the Convergence started."

Unsure, Mitch and Russ glanced back toward Bulldog. "What are you waiting for?" he roared.

They approached again. Dana lifted her hand up at one of the trees lining the clearing, and yelled a couple of words I didn't understand. A flash of light and a burst of flame forked across one of the branches. The branch severed from the tree and flew through the air toward where Mitch approached her. The wood smacked him square in the back, knocking him off balance. He went down heavily, smacking his head on one of the boulders surrounding the edges of one of the smaller pools. He lay there, unmoving.

Not letting the fall of his friend get to him, Russ attacked from the other side. He produced the weapon he'd been concealing, and pressed the muzzle at Dana's temple. "If any of you try anything witchy," he told Laurel and Kayla, "your leader gets it."

"The time's almost here, Riley," Bulldog yelled. From his belt, he produced the knife he'd threatened me with earlier. "You'd better get your vampire ready."

Riley reached out and took me by the arm, pulling me close to his body. He whispered in my ear, "I'm sorry."

"You will be," I hissed back, though my threats were unsubstantial. Unless I regained most of my strength in the next few minutes, I didn't know how I was going to get out of this alive.

I could feel the eyes of Laurel's circle on me, horror and a question in them. Vampire. Of course they'd heard Bulldog call me a vampire.

I glanced up at the sky. The stars were barely visible on either side of the moon now, the moon almost completely obscuring them. It would only be a matter of minutes, and the Convergence would begin.

And so would the hell cycle.

"Do your thing, Riley," Bulldog commanded.

Still with one hand holding me, he lifted out his other hand toward the water. A new wind whipped up, lifting leaves and dirt and branches from the ground, whipping our hair and clothes. But the main focus of the wind was the pool. It stirred its surface, creating only a circle of ripples at first, but those ripples quickly became waves, though they seemed to have no direction. Then I realized they did have a direction. It was up.

Riley created a spiral of air, lifting the water from the pool into the sky.

A tornado. He'd created a tornado to remove the water from the pool.

I could see the edges of the pool now, the water pulling away from the sides as it lifted higher. The sides were made of rock and dirt, but the lower it got, the more the material changed—a substance I didn't think I'd ever seen before. Black glass, but not. Glass which seemed to ripple and stir. Glass which seemed alive.

Something moved down there, and I gave a shriek and leaped back. Had I imagined it? No, I didn't think so.

Something humanoid, with long skeletal arms and legs, and a pale, naked scalp, appeared to be scaling the walls of the pool.

It wanted into Sage Springs, and I doubted it would be alone.

"Riley! Stop it! Stop it now!" I wrenched out of his grasp and took hold of him instead, shaking him. But he didn't lose control of his spell.

"You need to kill her now if this is going to work," said Riley, addressing The Bull. Then he pulled me back to him and spoke fast and low in my ear. "Don't be afraid. He can't hurt you."

Bulldog took a couple of steps toward me. I hesitated, looking between everyone here—Riley, Laurel's circle, even Brooke—and knew I couldn't run. I couldn't just leave them all here to face whatever was coming.

Bulldog took hold of my arm. Though I knew I couldn't escape, I couldn't resist swinging my elbow back and giving him a satisfying whack in the gut. He coughed and yanked me back harder, hurting my shoulder. "Little bitch," he said in my ear.

He could insult me all he wanted. It made no difference to me.

Across the pool, a figure stepped from between the trees. Broad shouldered, blond haired.

My heart jumped with happiness. "Flynn!"

"I told you he was trouble, Beth," he yelled at me. "You didn't listen."

"Do something and then lecture me," I shouted back. "You're supposed to be the protector of the pools. Where the hell were you?"

Bulldog gave my arm an extra yank. "Shut it, both of you. There's nothing you can do now. You'll both be dead in a matter of minutes."

Russ took the gun away from Dana's head and waved it in Flynn's direction. "Should I shoot him, Boss?"

Bulldog shook his head. "No, keep the gun on the girl."

The funnel of water grew higher. Almost all of the water from the pool was now suspended in the air. The creature I'd spotted before had made it halfway up the inside of the pool, and more movement came from below. I knew without a doubt that these were the things that would start the hell cycle.

"Do something, Flynn!" I cried.

He lifted his hands above his head, as if he was about to dive, but he didn't jump. Instead, he began to push his palms down in an arch. He appeared to be pressing against a force I couldn't see, but when I glanced up, I saw the funnel of water Riley had created beginning to get lower. Somehow, he was forcing the water back down.

Riley's concentration increased, his face taut with focus. With every bit of downward pressure Flynn applied, Riley's efforts doubled back. They were fighting each other. A battle I could only see by the elements involved.

Riley risked breaking his concentration for a moment to yell over an instruction to Bulldog. "Move closer. You need to hold her over the edge, so when her blood is spilled it pours into the pool. Her blood can't be spilled on our dirt."

Bull pushed me forward, the knife held against my throat. He leaned me closer over the edge, so I stared down into its vast, black depth. Dizziness spun over me. Feeling like I was falling already. Was that what he planned? He would slit my throat, and I would die plummeting into those depths. The last things I would ever experience were those strange glassy black walls and the feeling of falling.

I thought of my parents, how they'd kissed me goodbye, never knowing it was for the last time. I thought of the people of Sage Springs, and possibly even the rest of America, how their lives would change forever after this night. How the hell cycle was about to begin.

Several tons of water swirled above our heads. I felt as though I was looking up into an ocean. It was both overwhelming and terrifying. The pool was an empty black hole now, or not so empty. From its depths, more of the creatures emerged, their fingers long and spindly, with long, curled nails, or perhaps claws, protruding from the ends.

The creatures were getting closer, a couple of them only a matter of feet from the top. One reached up, its claws curling around the edge, digging into the grass and soil.

I tried one last time. "Please, Riley. Don't let him do this."

But the boy I'd fallen in love with ignored me.

His attention was focused on someone else.

Riley and Flynn exchanged a glance. I had enough time to think, 'What's going on there?' Then Riley shouted, "Now!"

My survival instinct kicked in. I shoved away from Bulldog, diving for the ground. The edge of the blade sliced across my throat with a sharp sting, but I didn't have time to worry about it. A roar came from above and suddenly ten tons of water collapsed on top of Bulldog's head.

He floundered, his arms spread out as though thin air could help him, and then the force of the water pummeled him down, his feet flying up into the air.

The water was back in the pool, sloshing from side to side from the motion.

His hand reached out of the surface for help, only for a black claw to reach up out of the water beside him and drag him back under.

"Never trust anyone," Riley said, addressing the water as he stood over the pool Bulldog had vanished into. He shook his head, sadly. "You taught me that, Bull."

CHAPTER 24

I LIFTED MY hand to my throat, expecting at any moment to start choking on my own blood from where the blade had punctured my windpipe. But when I brought my hand away, my palm was clean, and the choking never came. I frowned, confused. I'd felt the blade slit my skin and enter my flesh. Why wasn't I hurt?

Then I noticed the symbols Riley had drawn on me, all glowing in the dark, just like the time I'd seen them on Brooke in our room.

Riley crouched beside me and took the hand which I still stared at, perplexed. "I did a protective spell on you back at Bulldog's trailer," he said. "I didn't use the symbols to prepare you for the afterlife."

I managed to tear my eyes away from my palm and looked up at him. "You didn't?"

He gave a small smile. "You can't actually think I would ever let anyone hurt you?"

I opened my mouth and shut it again. I didn't know what to say. I had thought he was going to let someone hurt me. I'd thought he'd served me up and handed me to Bulldog Mackenzie on a platter.

A groan caught my attention, and Mitch started to shift, coming around. Russ reached down to help his friend to his feet. He tucked the gun back in his belt and lifted his hands in defense.

"We don't want no trouble," he said. "We were only doing what Bulldog told us. We ain't got no beef with all of you."

My first instinct was to kill the pair of them. They deserved to go the same way as Bulldog. Anger built within me, the familiar red haze descending on my vision. All of my muscles tightened, and I realized the herb they'd fed me had completely worn off.

I started forward, but Riley's hand on my arm stopped me. "Leave them," he said. "They're not worth it." He raised his voice. "Get out of here, or we'll get the cops onto you for abducting a college girl."

"You ain't no innocent in this either, Riley," Mitch yelled back. "What proof have you got that you weren't involved?"

Riley glanced to me, and I nodded.

"Witnesses," he replied. "I've got witnesses. What have you got?"

Russ and Mitch exchanged a glance and then turned their backs and ran off into the forest. I had to hold myself back from taking after them and hunting them down.

"Let them go," said Riley. "They don't have the brains to cause any more trouble."

Flynn approached us.

Without saying anything, I put my arms around him and squeezed him tight. He was warm, solid muscle beneath my touch, and I felt eternally grateful to have him here. I might not have the same feelings for him as he had for me, but without him, we wouldn't have won.

"Hi, Beth," he said, his face in my hair.

"Thank you," I told him, letting him go so I could stand back beside Riley.

He shrugged. "It wasn't just me. And anyway, it was his idea." He nodded toward Riley.

I looked between them, and frowned. "It was? But don't you hate him?"

"Just because I don't like him, doesn't mean I won't work with him. We're the same, remember?"

Riley gave a nonchalant shrug. "We knew Bulldog would need to believe everything was going to plan, and that he was winning. We couldn't make him think it was too easy. To be honest, though, we didn't think you'd be involved. We thought it was going to be Brooke."

Brooke heard her name. "Thought what was going to be me? What the hell are we doing out here anyway?"

Inspiration hit me. "You're sleepwalking, Brooke."

She blinked in surprise. "I am?"

"Yeah, you're a terrible sleepwalker." She looked horrified. "Don't worry, we'll keep it between us," I said with a smile.

She breathed out a sigh. "Oh, thank you. I'd hate for everyone to know."

Melissa let out a groan and started to open her eyes. Dana, Laurel, and Kayla were already at her side, and they helped her to sit up.

"Is she going to be okay?" I asked.

Dana nodded. "Yeah, now the Convergence is over, everything will go back to how it was."

I remembered the alignment and glanced up. The stars had passed across the back of the moon and had come out the other side. The moon itself was already smaller, and the blood red was only a tinge of color. I expected in another hour the moon would look almost normal.

"How did you guys know to be here?" I asked the circle. "Were you in on this plan Flynn and Riley had?"

Dana shook her head. "When you didn't come back, we went to the carnival, but the place was being broken down, and no one had seen you. Time was running out, and we figured that if what you'd told us about the Convergence was right, then this would be the place you'd be."

I smiled. "Thank you. It meant a lot to me seeing you all here. Sorry it might have gotten you killed."

"Well, you were right about the Convergence. Something bigger than a few spirits getting through was happening."

Suddenly, I remembered something. "Did any of them get out?" I asked in panic.

Dana frowned. "Any of what?"

"Those things! Those awful creatures with the claws and the long, skinny arms." I knew my description was barely brushing the surface of what they'd been. Something terrible, total darkness.

My friends exchanged worried glances. Dana put her hand on my arm. "I didn't see anything else, Beth."

"Maybe you weren't close enough. Could you even see into the hole from where you were?"

"Well, maybe not deep, but I could see some, yeah."

"But one of them was pulling itself out as the water came down. You must have seen it." They exchanged that glance again, and my shoulders sagged. "You didn't see it, did you? None of you did."

Riley shook his head. "Sorry, Icy."

Dammit.

"Look, we need to get Melissa home," said Dana. "Brooke, too. I guess we'll have to talk about the whole 'vampire' thing another time."

My cheeks colored. My secret was out. "Sure."

With their arms around each other for support, they walked away from the pools and back onto the trail.

Flynn looked between me and Riley. "Can I trust you to get her home safely?" he said to Riley.

Riley scowled. "Of course."

"Hey," I admonished. "What have I told you two about me not needing a babysitter?"

The corner of Flynn's mouth turned up. "Sorry. Well, as much as I enjoy playing gooseberry to the two of you, I think I'll make sure the other girls make it back to campus."

"Okay. And thanks, Flynn," I said again.

He shrugged. "No problem." And he turned his back and disappeared off after the girls.

Riley turned to me. "That all—"

I didn't give him a chance to finish. Instead, I shoved him in the chest, pushing him backward with my strength. He staggered back, his blue eyes wide with surprise.

"How could you do that?" I cried. "How could you betray me like that? You told Bulldog to kill me!"

"No, I didn't tell Bulldog to kill you because I wanted you dead. I was trying to buy time. If I hadn't given The Bull a reason to keep you alive, he would have killed you there and then."

A glimmer of light sparked my heart. Had Riley been planning on betraying Bulldog all along? But then I remembered something else. "But what about Brooke? You'd been preparing her for a sacrifice. You'd been doing magic on her." The idea that he might have seen Brooke naked, had touched her body in order to draw the runes on her skin, sent an absurd stab of jealousy racing through me.

"Bulldog told me no one would die. It was supposed to have been a little bloodletting spell to tie us to the magic in the pools at the right time. Bulldog wanted his own power. When I realized how far he planned on taking things, I turned to Flynn for help."

"It's still bad enough," I said, shaking my head, tears trembling in my vision. "That you would hurt anyone is bad enough."

"What, like you've never hurt anyone?" he challenged me.

I didn't know what to say. He was right. "I only hurt people who were asking for it."

"And you get to make that decision? Brooke and her family are far from innocent. They plunder the earth, tear nature to pieces in order to make their money. It's partly the mining that's caused the instability of the pools. She's tied to the land, she's part of it. She isn't so innocent, you know."

"Brooke's not responsible for her parents."

"No, you're right, she isn't." His voice grew softer. "So what about me, Icy? Bulldog and the others practically raised me. I did what I did because they asked me to, and I wanted to help them. It was only when you came on the scene that I started to ask myself if what they were doing was right. And then that night Jordy attacked you, I realized I cared about more than just the other carnies now." He looked at me, his eyes so deep, my tears mirrored in his own, pool-like depths. "I would never hurt you. I love you, Elizabeth. I've loved you from the very first moment you stepped onto the midway, when you caught my eye right before the accident. It was like you reached inside my chest and claimed my heart for your own."

"You love me?" My voice was a nervous stutter.

He nodded, his face utterly serious. "With every inch of my being."

I could hold back no longer. I threw myself in his arms.

"I love you, too," I managed, a muffled cry. He lifted my face and kissed me, ignoring the wet and the salt, kissing my pain away.

But then I remembered he was still leaving.

"What about the carnival?"

He shrugged. "I don't know. Now Bulldog's not running things, people may disband. Join other carnivals, I'm not sure."

"What about you?"

He reached out and stroked my hair from my face. "I'm not going anywhere. My home's right here with you."

My heart sung. Here we were, neither of us normal, neither perfect, but we'd found each other in this imperfect world.

Like what you've read? Book two in the Dhampyre Chronicles, *Twisted Magic*, will be released in 2015. Did you know The Dhampyre Chronicles is a spinoff of Marissa Farrar's dark vampire series, The Serenity Series? Why not check it out as the first book, *Alone*, is free across most book retailers!

Make sure you sign up to Marissa Farrar's new release list to stay updated about new releases, exclusives, and special offers! www.marissa-farrar.blogspot.com

ACKNOWLEDGEMENTS

I had some extra special help from some people during the writing of *Twisted Dreams*. As I have never been to an American college, I drew on the experiences of some of my wonderful online friends who were kind enough to answer my numerous questions! Those friends were Trina JamesKnerr, Ashley Dora, and Dyamone Gabrielle Rockmore. Thank you so much, ladies. Your insight and help was invaluable.

As always, I also want to thank my editor Lori Whitwam, who worked with her usual lightning fast accuracy, and spotted so many of my errors before I hung them out in public for all to see.

I would also like to thank Karri, who designed my cover art. It wasn't an intentional design, as I spotted this artwork when it won a competition and immediately knew I wanted it for Elizabeth's book. I can't wait to see what you come up with for book two!

Thank you, as well, to my little team of fantastic proofreaders, Glynis Elliott, AJ Wilcox, and Kim Hayes. I know Lori's excellent work doesn't often give you much to do, but your sharp eyes are need and appreciated nonetheless.

And finally, thank you to all my readers. Without you, all of these books would never get written.

Marissa

About the Author

Marissa Farrar is a multi-published fantasy and horror author. She was born in Devon, England, has travelled all over the world, and has lived in both Australia and Spain. She now resides in the countryside with her husband, three young children, a crazy Spanish dog, and two rescue cats. Despite returning to England, she daydreams of one day being able to split her time between her home country and the balmy, white sandy beaches of Spain.

Even though she's been writing stories since she was small and held dreams of being a writer, her initial life plan went a different way.

In her youth, inspired by James Herriot, she decided to become a vet, and would regularly bring home new pets to her weary parents. Upon discovering her exams were never going to get her into a veterinary degree, she ended up studying Zoology. Once she completed her degree and realised she'd spent the majority trying to find time to write, she decided to follow her dream of being an author. Seven years later, she was published and two years after that she was able to say goodbye to the day job.

However, she's continued to collect animals!

Marissa is the author of twelve novels, including the dark vampire 'Serenity' series. Her short stories have been accepted for a number of anthologies including, *Their Dark Masters*, Red Skies Press, *Masters of Horror: Damned If You Don't*, Triskaideka Books; and *2013: The Aftermath*, Pill Hill Press.

If you want to know more about Marissa, then please visit her website at www.marissa-farrar.blogspot.com.

You can also find her at her facebook page, www.facebook.com/marissa.farrar.author or follow her on twitter @marissafarrar.

She loves to hear from readers and can be emailed at marissafarrar@hotmail.co.uk.

Also by Marissa Farrar

The Serenity Series:

The Vengeful Vampire (free short story)
Alone (free first novel of the series!)
Buried
Captured
Dominion
Endless

The Spirit Shifters Series:

Autumn's Blood (free novel)
Saving Autumn
Autumn Rising
Autumn's War (out December 2014)

UNDERLIFE
(Please note, the prequel to Underlife, Go Back, is now free to download from Amazon)
THE DARK ROAD
WHERE THE DEAD LIVE
IN THE COMPANY OF THE DEAD
THE BODY FARM

THE SOUND OF CRICKETS (Women's Fiction Novel)

www.ingramcontent.com/pod-product-compliance
Lightning Source LLC
Chambersburg PA
CBHW020405150626
46554CB00012B/251

9780992850463